"I was thinking," Brady said slowly, "about cavemen."

Anya looked at him. "So, what were you thinking about cavemen?"

"That they had a very direct approach to life," Brady answered, and sat up abruptly. "Why don't you move over here? This rock is big enough for both of us, and it's more comfortable to lean back."

She made an incoherent sound of dismay as his hands slid underneath her arms and lifted her, swung her around, and sat her down beside him.

"Relax," he said. "It's no big deal."

Relax? With their shoulders touching and her insides melting?

"You didn't like it when I moved you over here, did you?" he asked soberly.

Anya swallowed. "It's all right," she said, valiantly casual. "You were just trying to make me comfortable."

The blue eyes glinted. "No, I wasn't. I was trying to get you close to me." The eyes went right on talking to her, moving slowly over her face, hesitating on her mouth . . .

Christa Merlin *is a native Floridian with an enduring love for saltwater and boats. A former newspaper columnist and editor, she finds romance writing fascinating. "I love the characters who arrive and seem to take over with a will of their own," she says. Christa is married and has two sons, a daughter, a golden retriever, and two Manx cats.*

Dear Reader:

October is here—and so are the newest SECOND CHANCE AT LOVE romances!

Kelly Adams has a special talent for endowing ordinary people with extraordinary warmth and appeal. In *Sunlight and Silver* (#292), she places such thoroughly likable characters in a dramatic love story set in America's heartland, on the Mississippi River. Riverboat captain Jacy Jones comes from a long line of women who know better than to trust high-handed men. Joshua Logan comes from a privileged background of wealth and breeding that's always set him apart. The battle of wills between these two *very* independent people sparks sensual shock waves that rival the currents in the ol' Miss!

Few writers create characters as warmly human and endearingly quirky as Jeanne Grant, winner of the Romance Writers of America's Silver Medallion award. In *Pink Satin* (#293), voluptuous lingerie consultant Greer Lothrop feels more comfortable playing the role of resident housemother to new neighbor Ryan McCullough than acting the femme fatale. But Ryan isn't about to accept chicken soup in lieu of tender loving kisses. Once again, Jeanne Grant demonstrates her superlative skill as a teller of love stories in a romance you'll treasure.

With the emotional honesty and sensitivity she is fast becoming beloved for, Romance Writers of America's Bronze Medallion winner Karen Keast touches our hearts with a story of forbidden love between divorcée Sarah Braden and her ex-husband's brother, cartoonist Cade Sterling. While she never shrinks from complex emotional issues, Karen dazzles us with her skillful use of male viewpoint, her lyrical prose—*and* her humor! I can't sing the praises of Karen Keast and *Forbidden Dream* (#294) loudly enough!

Love With a Proper Stranger (#295) by Christa Merlin is a powerful love story with an element of intrigue that will keep you breathlessly turning the pages. Anya Meredith doesn't think she's a candidate for a whirlwind romance, but Brady Durant teases and tantalizes her until she impulsively surrenders to passion. Yet when Brady is linked to a mystery surrounding an antique music box. Anya's trust in her lover is severely shaken. Don't miss this gripping romance written by the author of *Kisses Incognito* (#199).

For Anglophiles everywhere, Frances Davies's frolicsome pen creates an unabashedly romantic British drawing-room comedy (at times it's a little like a French bedroom farce, too!), complete with a cast of lovable eccentrics—including the hero, dazzling romance and mystery writer Andrew Wiswood. With witty one-liners and flights of sheer poetry, Frances whisks us to heather-covered Yorkshire and immerses us in whimsy. *Fortune's Darling* (#296) is a sophisticated, delectable romp.

In *Lucky in Love* (#297) Jacqueline Topaz once again creates a bright, breezy romance that will make you feel good all over. Cheerfully unconventional exercise instructor Patti Lyon is willing to bet she can take the starch out of staunch civic leader Alex Greene. But Patti's game-show winnings and laidback lifestyle don't convince Alex to support legalized gambling. In the bedroom he's mischievously eager to play games ... but elsewhere he intends to show her there's more to life than fun and frolic!

Until next month, enjoy! Warm wishes,

Ellen Edwards

Ellen Edwards, Senior Editor
SECOND CHANCE AT LOVE
The Berkley Publishing Group
200 Madison Avenue
New York, NY 10016

Second Chance at Love.

LOVE WITH A PROPER STRANGER
CHRISTA MERLIN

SECOND CHANCE AT LOVE
BOOK

Second Chance at Love books are published by
The Berkley Publishing Group
200 Madison Avenue, New York, NY 10016

LOVE WITH A
PROPER STRANGER

Chapter 1

THE FIRST THING Anya Meredith noticed about the man entering Postons' Art and Antiques Shop was his hurried stride and the quick, sweeping glance he gave the small antique bibelots in the glass wall case. That stride and glance brought her to her feet. She smoothed down her skirt as she came around the counter, and went toward him with a bright, professional smile. Even her short experience had taught her to watch for a man in a hurry for a last-minute gift. In the tiny resort town of Helen, Georgia, the buying customer was king. There was fierce competition along the single street of shops.

The man was staring at the contents of the glass case as Anya approached, which gave her a chance to size him up. She was surprised by her first reaction—that tiny jolt of female instinct, that awareness a woman feels when she sees an attractive man. Why? Not his clothes— the usual worn jeans, plaid shirt, and boots so many of the local populace wore. Maybe the lean, tall body, the rumpled black hair, the profile too rugged to be handsome. Anyway, there was something...

"May I help you?"

Black brows shot upward as he turned. "Well, hello, there! I expected Mrs. Poston."

So, he was a friend or acquaintance of her cousin, Marilee Poston. Anya's smile went from professional to friendly. "Marilee will be in this afternoon if you need special help..." She had been planning to say more, but a totally illogical sense of recognition, a feeling of familiarity, had swept through her as she met his gaze. His

1

eyes were a deep, bright blue in a roughly carved, lined face, framed by thick lashes beneath those heavy brows, and they looked into hers with a startled expression as if he, too, was wondering where they had met. But she was sure she had never seen him before, and he didn't resemble anyone else she knew. So, what was it? Conscious that she was staring, she glanced away, adding quickly, "Mrs. Poston knows the stock much better than I do. If you'd like to wait . . . ?"

"You'll do just fine." He sounded as if he meant it.

Anya stared at the shelves with an air of studied thoughtfulness. Small antique figurines of bisque, hand-cut crystal bells and vases, and gold and silver music boxes stared back at her. She hardly saw them. She was trying to deal with a brand-new sensation. Invisible antennae seemed to be wavering in the air between this man and herself, reaching and touching lightly, like airy octopi.

"What do you have in mind?" Now, why did that simple question suddenly sound provocative? Only your own overheated imagination, she told herself angrily.

"Well," the man said, a touch of laughter in his voice, "when I came in, I was looking for something small and expensive."

"We have many things that are small and expensive," Anya said shortly, keeping her eyes on the shelves. "Can you be more specific?" She could feel those blue eyes appraising her. Well, he'd find nothing exciting. Only a thirty-one-year-old woman with plain brown hair and green eyes too big for her face. A decent figure, maybe, but hardly tantalizing in the straight skirt, oversized shirt, and medium-heel pumps she wore in the shop. Bothered by his silence, she glanced back in time to see his gaze traveling slowly up to her face again. He grinned, and white, even teeth made the rugged face look enormously appealing.

"Yes, I think I can be very specific. What I'm after is something you probably wouldn't like."

"Wouldn't like?" Anya was sure she had misunderstood.

"Exactly." His face still crinkled by the grin, he swung to look at the shelves again. "Think of a blonde. A beautiful little blonde with a taste for rare, expensive things. A lady who has already acquired everything she wants."

That was easy. Anya thought of Charlotte Martin. No, Charlotte Meredith, now. The description fit. Blond, small, and beautiful, Charlotte had everything she wanted—including Tom Meredith, Anya's ex-husband. Anya's softly contoured mouth compressed. It had been almost a year since the divorce, and she hadn't thought of Tom and his gorgeous Charlotte in months, until this man had reminded her. She watched somberly as he pushed back the glass door of the case and reached in for an ornately carved silver music box. Then she smiled slightly.

"I think you've found it, sir. It's small, very expensive, and I don't like it."

"'Sir'?" He laughed, taking the music box from its place, turning it over and examining it. "I'm Brady Durant, Miss . . . ?"

"Mrs.," Anya corrected stiffly. "Mrs. Meredith." She waited, sure that he would put the box back in its place and leave the shop. The price was on the bottom and she didn't think him fool enough to pay eight hundred dollars for a trinket. She watched the long fingers trace the deep, elaborate carving of flowers and vines that embellished the box. The fingers looked strong, the nails clipped close and clean; there was a smudge of azure blue paint on one knuckle. She surmised that he was one of the many amateur painters who frequented the mountains around Helen.

"Why does it cost so much?" he asked casually. "It doesn't even play a tune."

Silently, Anya reached over and twisted one of the intricate roses on the side of the box. Immediately, the tinkling strains of a Chopin piano étude filled the air. Durant looked at her and laughed, catching the subtle challenge in her green eyes. "That's worth eight hundred dollars?"

"Not to me," Anya said recklessly. "I wouldn't have it as a gift. It's—pretentious. Too small to be useful, and as for the sound, I've heard better music from crickets."

He laughed again. He had a nice laugh, deep and infectious. Anya's smile broke out, genuine this time.

"I meant that, Mr. Durant. But I'm not a collector. A collector would know it's worth more than its price. It's one of a kind, made by the famous Jacob Bruner, with his initials and benchmark on the left side. Also, it's 94.2 percent solid silver, a better grade than sterling, and it's over a hundred and fifty years old. Marilee ordered it from France on a written request from a collector."

Durant's gaze moved up from the costly toy in his hands and met her eyes squarely again, the warmth of his glance replaced by a cool curiosity. "If it was ordered for a collector, why is it for sale?"

The look jolted Anya. It was as if the sky had narrowed down into a blue laser beam that cut through all her defenses and probed for her innermost thoughts.

"Because the man never came for it," she blurted out, "or answered her letters. In fact, the letters came back, marked 'address unknown.' So Marilee put it on the shelf and brought the price down. It's still too expensive for our usual trade, but at eight hundred she's only breaking even..." She stopped, flushing, and added lamely, "I know how that last remark sounds, but it's the truth."

The laser beam went away and the grin came back. "I believe you," Durant said solemnly. "One thing you aren't is a hard-sell saleslady." He handed her the box. "I'll take it. It's perfect."

Anya stood there, shocked and awkward, as he reached for his wallet and handed her a MasterCard. Then she walked dazedly back to the counter, listening to his footsteps following. Marilee was going to be ecstatic. Neither she nor her husband, Roger, thought they would ever get their money out of the Bruner box. They didn't have the right connections, and collectors for antique music boxes were few and far between.

"I'll gift-wrap it for you," she offered, handing him the slip to sign, feeling an excited sense of triumph as she watched him scrawl a spiky black signature. "Oh, I forgot to show you how it opens." She reached for the box again and touched a tiny hidden catch beneath the carved rose. The lid sprang up, revealing a padded red velvet interior. "It has a secret compartment, too." She lifted the padded interior out. Under it was a very small space lined with polished rosewood and completely empty. "If your wife, or friend, has a very small secret, she can hide it there." Excitement had put a sparkle in her emerald green eyes, a flush on her cheeks, and her lips were parted breathlessly as she fitted the music box into its own velvet-lined container for shipping. As she leaned against the counter, her position had tightened the loose shirt over shapely, rounded breasts. Durant's eyes roved over her warmly.

"I don't have a wife," he said deliberately. "It's for my sister-in-law." He glanced at his wristwatch and then back at her face. "By the time you finish wrapping that, it'll be noon. Will you have lunch with me?"

Anya wanted to say yes, and that surprised her. It wasn't uncommon in the relaxed, vacation air of this village for male shoppers to ask Anya out, as if they thought they deserved a little extra attention for buying the expensive gifts. Anya had always refused, usually laughing and saying, "It's *Mrs.* Meredith, sir. Sorry." But Durant already knew that, and it hadn't stopped him. Maybe he was just being friendly, but she didn't think so. Her delicate brows drew together slightly. She still wasn't ready for even a mild flirtation, especially with a man as attractive and compelling as this one.

"Thank you," she said, putting a touch of coolness in her voice, "but I don't get off until one, and I have a busy afternoon ahead of me."

"You still have to eat," he said easily. "I'll come back." He watched as she silently folded silver paper around the package, her slim hands precise, then fastened a single long-stemmed pink silk rose along the top. He smiled. "Nice touch." He picked the package up and nodded at her. "See you at one o'clock." He didn't wait for an answer.

Her brows together again, Anya stared after him as he crossed the busy street with that long-limbed stride, opened the door of a huge dark green van, and tossed the package in, climbing in after it. She shuddered, thinking of the delicate mechanism in that Bruner. Well, it was his now. But she wasn't, not even for lunch. Marilee, who was supposed to be in by twelve, would arrive as usual at twelve-thirty. And Marilee was very good at explaining why her cousin, Anya, who was only helping out temporarily in the shop, had to leave early.

Marilee came dashing in at exactly twelve-thirty, wearing a colorful red and green calico country dress and apologizing profusely for being late. She was thirty-five, thin, excitable, and enthusiastic. Untamed spikes of black curls stood out around a face dominated by round brown eyes and a winning smile.

"It's inevitable!" she exclaimed. "This time, Sarah fell down the steps and bruised her chin. At least, I think it was Sara ... Anyway, I had to carry her in and comfort her ... Why are you laughing, you rat? Poor little Sara— or was it Susan?"

Anya straightened her face with an effort. "I would say Sara, unless the child in question also had a bruise on her forehead. Susan ran into the library table yesterday, don't you remember? It was Sara's turn." Anya laughed again as Marilee spread her hands and grimaced helplessly. The Poston twins, at two and a half, were the youngest of five Poston children, and by far the most time-consuming. Anya had extended her visit to the Postons to fill in at the shop while Marilee tried out new baby-sitters. The twins had worn out the last one. "How's the new sitter?" she asked, changing the subject diplomatically.

"Great, if she'll stay. She doesn't like being out so far in the country." Marilee unslung the heavy shoulder bag that rested on her thin arm and dropped it behind the counter. "Lord, it's so peaceful here. Too peaceful, I guess." She sighed and looked around the empty shop. "Business as usual in September, I suppose. Slow."

The perfect opening. Anya smiled and spared no time or detail in telling Marilee about the sale of the Bruner music box. Marilee's jaw dropped, and her round eyes grew rounder. Anya could have sworn the black curls vibrated. "I threw in one of those expensive silk roses," she ended airily, "to dress up the package."

"You should have thrown in a dozen," Marilee gasped, dancing up and down. "It would have been worth it. How did you dare say all those negative things? But who cares? It worked!" She collapsed in a chair, laughing. "No matter how you did it, cuz, you've made my day, my week, my month! I had begun to hate that box."

Anya smiled, picking up her own handbag, a neat, conservative affair of gray suede. "Fortunately, I didn't like it, either. Now, you will tell him I couldn't wait for the lunch date he thinks he has with me, won't you?"

"He asked you out? You bet I will! I'll tell him you have a two-hundred-pound insanely jealous husband. I want you to start dating, but not with a nut like that. What's his name?"

Anya thought. "Brady Durant, he said."

Marilee shot upward in her chair. "Anya! Brady Durant is no nut!" Her attitude changing rapidly, Marilee's face took on a look of cunning. "Listen, stay and have lunch with him. You know how weak we are in the art department—nothing but prints and amateur watercolors. Think what we could do with Durant's paintings."

Bewildered, Anya hesitated. "I know nothing about art," she began, and, as usual, Marilee interrupted her.

"You just know what you don't like?" Marilee giggled

and jumped up, beginning to pace and wave her hands at the walls. "Look what we have hanging—who wants them? With Durant's mountain scenes on our walls, we'd have tourists climbing up after them. So far, Brady just sells out of his van at ridiculously low prices. The other shops have offered him space to hang and twice the money, but he always refuses. If he likes you..."

"No."

It wasn't like Anya to interrupt. Marilee frowned. "What?"

"I said no," Anya repeated. "I don't like him." That wasn't quite true. "I mean, I don't want to get to know him." Maybe that wasn't quite true either. "I don't feel I'm ready to—to get involved with a man." Now *that* was true.

"Listen," Marilee said intensely, widening her brown eyes, "he's perfect for you."

"So, anything I don't like is perfect, is it?" Anya asked wildly. "You have the same opinion of my taste as he does."

"I only meant," Marilee went on, clearly trying to sound reasonable, "that he's single, around the right age, very nice-looking, and an interesting, creative person. Considerably better than that unimaginative clod who threw you over for a sex-symbol blonde."

"Mr. Durant bought that music box for a blonde," Anya said. "He described her, and I would have sworn he was talking about Charlotte. What does that tell you?"

Marilee sighed and sprawled down into the chair again. "It tells me to shut up." She gave Anya a small smile. "It was a good idea while it lasted. When he comes in, I'll brace him myself about the paintings."

"Good," Anya agreed, "you do that." She was slightly ashamed of herself for not adding that the blonde was Durant's sister-in-law, but she knew from experience how hard it was to convince Marilee in an argument. Anya would still have been at the shop at one o'clock if she hadn't been a bit deceptive. She left, going out onto the wide sidewalk and making her way through the huge, flower-laden redwood boxes that took up half of it. She turned through the crowd toward the parking lot, where she kept her car.

Even after weeks, Anya wasn't used to the imitation Alpine village around her. Helen was a town of peaked roofs and gay banners, of cobbled little alleys and a European air. Every shop had its window boxes overflowing with colorful flowers, its tiny paned windows, and its specialties, ranging from mountain crafts to Viennese chocolates. A piece of Disney World, dropped down in the steep foothills of northern Georgia. But all around the small and highly competitive tourist attraction were the quiet reaches of mountains and forests, and that Anya did like. Relaxing, she walked slower, debating whether to go back to the Poston house for lunch, or to go for the gusto in the Bavarian Food Stall across the street, always crowded with tourists. Raising her eyes to the green distances, she thought with longing that what she would really like would be a picnic in the woods. Sitting on the bank of a mountain stream with a friend . . .

"There you are." Out of the flow of strangers around her, a hand grasped her arm, a tall body hovered over her. She looked up at the glint of sun on black hair, a blue gaze, and a charming grin. She silently cursed her luck and wished Brady Durant would take his persistent antennae elsewhere. They were making her skin tingle. "Lucky I saw you," Durant added, amused. "I would have missed you at the shop, wouldn't I? Trying to escape me, Mrs. Meredith?"

Anya struggled with a blush and lost. He was carrying a bag marked with the colorful insignia of the Bavarian Food Stall, and the aromas coming from it were mouth-watering. *He* was mouth-watering. He was even more attractive out here than he had been in the shop, as if the sunlight and clear mountain air were his natural elements. She felt again that disturbing familiarity, even more pronounced by his warm, hard hand on her arm. She forced herself to frown.

"How do you know I'm not meeting a two-hundred-pound, insanely jealous husband? Or don't you care?"

The grin quirked up at one side of his mouth. "I would say you don't have a husband at present, or you'd be wearing a ring. Some women don't, but you would. Or am I wrong?"

Anya wished she could lie. "No, you aren't wrong," she admitted weakly. "I don't have a husband at present, but I do have plans."

"To marry?" He was still smiling, still amused. Anya fought to suppress a smile but lost again. It could have sounded like that, and it was suddenly funny. If there was anyone who didn't have plans to marry, it was Anya Meredith. "No, just plans to go shopping."

"That settles it," Durant said, and turned her toward the huge van, half a block away. "You can't brave the crowds here on an empty stomach. Even the places to eat have double lines today. We're going on a picnic. I know a place with a stream . . ."

Recognizing the hand of fate, Anya gave in gracefully. Why argue when it was exactly what she wanted . . . except that this man wasn't her friend. In fact, she thought as she tried to match his stride, friendliness was about the only emotion she hadn't yet felt in his presence.

"Nice," she said a minute later, settling down in a big bucket seat. As Durant went around to get in the other side, she glanced back through the well-outfitted interior behind her. A tiny kitchenette, a table, a lot of storage space, and two built-in couches across from each other that probably made up into a bed. A *bed*? She glanced at him warily as he got in.

"Your home away from home?"

"Right," he said easily, and swung through to the kitchenette to put the bag exuding the delicious aromas in the tiny sink. Coming back, folding his long body into the driver's seat, he started the engine. "I live in this in the summers, traveling the mountains. I paint, mostly landscapes." He looked at her and smiled slowly. "I'd like to paint you."

"Really?" Anya asked, poker-faced. "What color?"

He burst into laughter, his craggy face creasing, and eased the heavy van out into traffic. "Pink, probably. I like it when you blush." His left hand came over and enclosed her fingers in that hard warmth. "I like *you,* Mrs. Meredith. Are you going to tell me your first name?"

Blush-pink? Anya's lips curved uncontrollably, her spirits rising. The man's warmth and charm were irresistible. She was actually having fun with a man again, when she thought she'd forgotten how in the last nine years. She leaned back, curling silken legs half under her, smoothing her skirt over them. "A small price for a picnic, Mr. Durant. My name is Anya."

"Anya," he said, testing it, almost tasting it. "Unusual, which suits you." They were out of the tiny town almost immediately, accelerating smoothly as the road twisted upward, the engine responding with the characteristic whine and clatter of a diesel. Shifting gears, he looked over at her again. "Isn't it Russian?"

Anya laughed softly. She certainly wasn't going to tell him her imaginative mother had named her after two aunts, Anne and Tanya. She turned so the fresh air blew against her face, lifting her hair from her neck, ruffling the open collar of her shirt. It felt wonderful, clean and crisp. "I'm a spy," she said, "planted here to wrest state secrets from unsuspecting tourists. Stupid of me to blow my cover by telling you my name."

Durant laughed with her, glancing at the delicate tip of an ear, the slender neck exposed by the blowing hair. All he could see of her face was the corner of her lips, still curving upward, the smile-rounded cheek, the long, dark lashes and winging tip of brow. "I have a feeling," he said, "that I'll tell you all my secrets as soon as you ask."

Anya was still watching the side of the mountain whirling past, thinking how quickly this part of the country went from civilized to primeval. "Then tell me how far we're going."

The van swerved slightly as Durant hugged the side of the mountain, watching a huge semi come screaming around the curve ahead, deafening them as it passed. "Five miles—maybe six," he said when the noise died away. "You'll like it."

She thought how positive he sounded. As if he had known her for years and had all her likes and dislikes catalogued in his mind. She glanced at him again. He was concentrating on his driving now, his tanned, rough face intent on the narrow road, his black hair ruffled by the wind. Her gaze ran over the wide, rangy shoulders, slid down the chest outlined by plaid wool. There wasn't an ounce of fat apparent anywhere on him. His waist was lean, his belly almost concave in the worn jeans, his hips narrow and muscular, virile-looking . . . She dropped her gaze hastily to the long, taut legs and the booted feet on the pedals. Then she looked away, biting the soft underside of her lower lip. She hated feeling vulnerable to a man, and, somewhere inside, she definitely felt vulnerable to this one.

Staring from the window, Anya wondered idly if she had married Tom Meredith merely because she had never felt vulnerable to him. He had been calm and sensible, an older man who talked about his golf game and grew roses in the backyard. Life with Tom had been pleasant and sexually adequate, but, as long as she could remember—and she'd known Tom all her life—he had never thought much about passion until he met Charlotte. Then he had thought of nothing else.

"I have to have her," he had said, shamed but resolute. "It's different, Anya. Real passion! I didn't know it existed."

Anya had hated breaking up a decent marriage, and Tom had hated that part, too.

"I'm so sorry," he had said, over and over. "We've always been such good friends."

Well, they still were. Anya had given him his freedom with little regret and no pain. That, she thought, was the value of not being vulnerable. She glanced again at Brady Durant with that same tiny jolt of awareness she had felt when she saw him first, and this time her instinct went further, informing her sagely to be wary. This was not a man to take lightly. A shiver that was both exciting and disturbing traveled the length of Anya's spine, and she suddenly knew she couldn't take Brady Durant lightly if she tried.

Chapter 2

THE ROAD AHEAD curved and then dropped, spiraling downward in a steep descent. Durant slowed and shifted gears expertly.

"A lot of weight in this baby," he commented as Anya sat up and glanced at him. "I like to be careful." He smiled, and Anya wondered if he knew how engaging that grin of his was. Probably. She concentrated on the road, which seemed to slip beneath them like a striped snake coiling its way up the mountain.

"How much farther?"

"The turnoff is just ahead," he replied, slowing again. "Then, maybe a mile."

The turnoff proved to be nothing more than a drop down into a shallow ditch, then up the other side to a gap in the thick woods and an indistinct trail barely wide enough for the van. In minutes, even the semblance of a trail was gone, and they plunged along over a thick carpet of leaves, avoiding impassable thickets and keeping to open places the van could negotiate. Anya clutched the door and thought what a fool she was to be here with a stranger. What Marilee had said about him was only vaguely comforting. "An interesting, creative person." Highly creative when it came to choosing picnic sites. Anya wondered if she could scream loudly enough to be heard a mile away. The van topped a forested rise and went grumbling down a steep incline toward what seemed to be an entirely new wilderness of big trees.

"Do you ever get stuck in this monster?" Anya noted

with scorn that her voice was high and shaky, that the damnable amusement was back in his face.

"Not often. She's got four-wheel-drive and a lot of power. Then, I have a winch, and there's always a tree. Hook her up right and she'll pull herself out. Anyway, we won't get stuck here. This is easy country."

To get lost in, Anya added to herself. There was a rearview mirror on her side, and she stared into it. Nothing familiar showed up behind. Only a disturbed swirl of leaves. She wondered how long it would be before the breeze restored them, making it impossible to find the way out.

The van stopped. "Just a short walk now," Durant said, and stood up, turning to the back of the van. He took the bag from the sink and handed it to her. "You carry that, and I'll get the rest."

Silently, Anya sat with the bag in her lap and watched him rummage a blanket from under a couch, open the door of a small refrigerator, and take out a six-pack of beer. Last, he lifted two glasses from a fenced shelf above and grinned at her. "All set. Can you get out by yourself?"

She nodded. Opening the door, she climbed down on trembling legs and looked at the big trees in front of them.

"In *there?*"

Coming around the front of the van, Durant laughed. "You aren't frightened, are you?"

"Oh, no," Anya lied. "It's just that I keep thinking of—of bears." Two lies in a row. What was she thinking had nothing to do with bears. She looked down at her legs in the sheer stockings, at her feet in the scooped-out pumps. "I'm not certain I can hike around in the woods in these."

"Sure you can. Just follow me." He set off confidently, and Anya followed with haste. It was better than staying alone.

It wasn't bad at all. The trees were big enough to

have shaded out the underbrush, and there was a thick carpet of leaves that cushioned her steps, then sunlight ahead and the sound of water running over rocks. They came out to a mossy slope of bank and a wide, clear stream that tumbled down a terraced fall of rocks far up to the right and rushed past them to disappear into a tunnel of lacy, pale green willows on the left. Anya stood entranced, the bag forgotten in her arms, and watched the sunlight flicker and gleam on the shallow water, watched a leaf swirl by with its shadow following along below, dancing on the rocky bottom.

"It's beautiful here." She sounded surprised, and Durant laughed. He had put the beer in a cleft in the rocks, half submerged in the icy water, and was spreading the blanket on the moss.

"I told you you'd like it."

Anya faced toward him. "What makes you think you know me so well, Mr. Durant?"

"Brady."

She smiled, mostly because she couldn't help it. "Brady, then. What makes you think you know me so well, Brady?"

He came to her, his black hair glinting in the sun like a raven's wing, his blue eyes as warm as a summer day. Reaching, he lifted the bag from her arms and stood looking down at her thoughtfully. "I'm not sure. Call it instant recognition. You go somewhere you've never been before, and yet you remember it. You meet a stranger, and it's as if you've known her forever. Hasn't it ever happened to you?"

Sensation chased along Anya's spine, tightened her throat. She turned away from the too-penetrating blue gaze and stared again at the swift-running stream. Not for the world would she admit to the same feeling of familiarity. "It couldn't happen to me," she said, making it light. "Until I came here, I had always lived in the same small town. Everyone I met I really *had* known forever." She felt very small herself, huddling behind her defenses, frightened by the uncontrollable attraction she felt for this unconventional man.

"And now everyone is a stranger?" Brady asked.

His voice had been gently teasing, as if he had known in spite of her how she felt. She had to break this mood. She moved away, her leather shoes slipping slightly on the mossy incline. "Everyone but Marilee and Roger," she said. "Marilee is my cousin. I stayed to help in the shop while she found a new baby-sitter." She had come, and stayed, because she couldn't bear being a discarded wife in a small town, but that was hard to admit even to herself. "Anyway," she added recklessly, "I'm leaving for New York, where I don't know anyone at all. That should be exciting, don't you think?"

"What I think," Brady said, taking her hand and pulling her back up on the bank to the blanket, "is that I'd better make it so exciting here that you won't want to leave. I don't meet a woman I've known forever every day. In fact," he added, putting the bag down and turning her to face him, "I've never met one I know as well as I know you. I think—no, I'm sure—I even know how it's going to be when I kiss you."

Jolted to her toes, Anya pulled away. "If that's a come-on," she said, shakily sarcastic, "it's not a very good one." She sat down on the blanket as far from him as she could manage and reached for the bag. "If you know me so well," she added, desperately trying for lightness, "you'd know I'm starving." She hardly knew what she was saying. Just for a moment there, she could actually feel his mouth closing on hers. It hadn't been real, but the liquid warmth in her belly, the tingling of her skin, they were real enough. She pulled a long, crusty roll from the bag and looked at it disbelievingly.

"Bavarian *heroes?*"

Brady laughed, dropping down across from her and reaching for the bag. "Inside they're Bavarian. Westphalian ham, smoked cheese, sausage, and sauerkraut. Great with beer." Reminded, he got up again and brought

beers for them both, handing her a glass and sitting back
down again. He leaned back, fitting his shoulders against
a convenient boulder, and began crunching into the crusty
roll. Eating, he watched Anya as if he enjoyed the sight
as much as the food. She sat primly on the blanket, her
slim legs drawn up in that characteristic way, tucked
halfway beneath her. The sun brought out chestnut high-
lights in her thick hair, and her eyes glistened leaf-green
beneath her long lashes. But she knew she looked thoroughly out of place in the long-sleeved blouse, straight
gray skirt, silk stockings, and pumps, and somehow that
seemed to add to Brady's enjoyment. He had snatched
her out of her element and brought her into his, a triumph
of sorts. Like a caveman dragging the female he fancied
into his cave.

"What are you grinning about?" Anya sounded suspicious. He looked so comfortable, stretched out on the
blanket and leaning against that rock. And so male. There
was a faint shadow of beard under the tanned skin, a
curl of black hair in the V of his opened shirt. She could
see muscles ripple under the plaid shirt as he reached for
his beer, and the hard lines of his long legs were clearly
defined by jeans that clung like a second skin. If we were
lovers, she thought suddenly, I would be beside him,
leaning on his shoulder. We'd be talking, laughing . . .
touching. Hurriedly, she took a bite of her sandwich and
filled her glass with beer. "Well?" she demanded. "Are
you going to tell me?"

"I was thinking," Brady said slowly, "about cavemen."

Anya looked at him over the rim of her glass, let the
refreshing bitterness run down her throat, and then lowered the glass for a better look. "So, what were you
thinking about cavemen?"

"That they had a very direct approach to life," Brady
answered, and sat up abruptly, startling her. "Why don't
you move over here? This rock is big enough for both
of us, and it's more comfortable to lean back."

"I'm fine," she said quickly and stared, fascinated,

as he rolled up on his knees and reached for her. She made an incoherent sound of dismay as his hands slid underneath her arms and lifted her, swung her around, and sat her down beside him. Beer slopped over the edge of her glass and left a trail of wet, dark spots on the blanket; a sliver of ham fell from her sandwich and dropped on her skirt.

"Now, look what you did," she said weakly, and stared again, amazed, as he deftly retrieved the ham, popped it into her half-open mouth, and began scrubbing at the greasy stain on her skirt with a paper napkin. The pressure on her upper thigh seemed much too intimate, and the way he leaned over her with his dark cheek inches from her mouth was unnerving. She caught his scent, a pleasant tang of light lotion mixed with the subtle aphrodisiac of warm male skin, and her body reacted without warning. Heat exploded in her middle and spread like wildfire, darting a teasing flame to her loins, reaching up to catch the breath in her throat and invading her breasts, drawing the small nipples into tiny points of fire.

"Give me that," she mumbled around the mouthful of ham. "I'll do it." She could feel the heat mounting to her face as she snatched the napkin and wriggled away, keeping her face averted and giving the small stain a great deal of attention. Naturally, the spot of grease remained. In a moment, Brady took the napkin gently and pulled her back against the rock.

"Relax. It's no big deal."

Relax? With their shoulders touching and her insides melting? Anya drew a deep breath and leaned back, smoothing down her rumpled skirt, crossing her nylon-clad ankles neatly.

"Of course," she said breathlessly. "Silly to make a fuss about such a small thing." She began eating, chewing and then swallowing, hard, past the tight place in her throat. She couldn't believe what had happened inside her. True, thirteen months on her own was a long time after nine years of marriage. And, this lanky charmer was obviously big league in the most popular indoor sport, but she had never—not even in the first year with Tom, when physical love had been such a pleasant surprise—*never* felt such a tremendous shock of sexual desire. She tried to think of something else and failed. His shoulder moved warmly against hers as he raised his glass to drink; his scent was faint but still tantalizing. She sat there in a rigid imitation of ease, afraid to turn and look at him. She was not, she told herself firmly, going to fling herself into the arms of the first attractive stranger she had met since her divorce.

A tanned hand and muscular arm reached across her, scooped up her half-empty glass, and disappeared in his direction. In a moment, the hand appeared again and set the glass down full, topped with an inch of foam above the amber liquid. The sides of the glass were beaded with cold droplets, and Anya reached for it gratefully. After a while, she laid aside her half-eaten sandwich and held the glass in both slim hands, glad for the chill.

"Too much for you?"

She nodded numbly, the wings of dark hair sliding forward to hide her face. Both the sandwich and the man who had bought it were too much for her. "It's very good, though," she said politely. "I suppose I just wasn't very hungry."

With one finger, Brady drew back the curtain of hair nearest himself and hooked it behind a small ear. His palm closed on her chin and turned her face to his. Anya looked at him like a fledgling bird would look at a cat, all eyes and ruffled feathers, hypnotized.

"You didn't like it when I moved you over here, did you?" he asked soberly.

Anya swallowed, her throat brushing spasmodically against his little finger. "It's—all right," she said, valiantly casual. "You were just trying to make me comfortable."

The blue eyes glinted. "No, I wasn't. I was trying to get you close to me. Do you mind?" The eyes went right on talking to her, moving slowly over her face, hesitating on her mouth.

Once again Anya's insides quivered with a frightened desire. But this time, a small, cold voice yammered at her hysterically. Brady Durant was very, very good at this. *Too* good. An expert at the game. Had he picked out a lonely divorcée for an afternoon's diversion, and was he now drawing in for the kill? The rough texture of the blanket beneath her reminded her he had made it all very convenient. An isolated, beautiful spot, food, beer, the blanket—and his own devastating charm. She forced herself to turn her face away, her chin twisting in his hand.

"Perhaps I do mind," she said, strangled. "It seems to me it's a bit early for this."

For another moment, he stared at her, then evasively turned her cheek and let her go. "If it takes time, we'll give it time," he said, and drew away from her. Leaning forward, he began taking off his boots. "Do Russians like wading in icy-cold water? Of course they do; they don't know there's any other kind. Get those shoes and stockings off. This stream will remind you of Siberia."

"I can't," Anya said, looking at the glittering stream and thinking that she probably would like it. "I really can't. You go ahead."

"Why can't you?" He paused, one foot bare, and looked around at her. His foot was long and well shaped, with a strong arch and tiny, springing black hairs on the toes. Anya flushed and looked away, staring down at her own legs.

"These aren't just stockings," she said. "They're pantyhose."

Brady erupted into laughter. "What difference does that make? They'll still come off, and your skirt will stay on."

"I'd rather not," she said stubbornly. She could, though. She could go behind a tree or a rock and wiggle out of them. The icy-clear water looked delightful, a cure for overheated blood. "But do go on. I'll sit here in the sun and have another beer." She didn't even like beer that much.

Brady shrugged and leaned forward to take off the other boot. His shirt strained down his long torso and across the muscled shoulders. His black hair shone, and Anya wondered how it felt—springing and coarse, or soft to the touch. Thick—you could bury a hand in it . . .

Standing, Brady wiggled his toes luxuriously in the moss and grinned down at her. "I could show you a trout or something," he said coaxingly.

She waved him off, snapping open a beer with a show of high spirits, and then watched jealously as he stepped into the stream, shivered, and waded away. He was half-way to the terraced, splashing falls when she kicked off her pumps and wiggled out of her pantyhose. Dropping the silky handful on the blanket, she set off after him, the bare skin of her hips and thighs feeling oddly free and unfettered beneath the tailored skirt. She gasped at the chill that shot upward from her slender feet as she stepped in and then went on, slipping and sliding over the rounded, water-slick stones on the bottom, avoiding the deeper pools near the big rocks. Looking ahead, she saw that Brady had stopped and was waiting for her.

"I changed my mind," she said unnecessarily, and, with a childlike gesture of trust, put her hand in his. "I decided I—I wanted to see a trout."

He looked down at her, his craggy face half shadowed by the sunlight on his hair, half lit by the reflection from the water below, his blue eyes intent and his wide mouth relaxed and tender. "Of course you do," he said softly. "Why miss anything? Maybe I can show you how the Indians used to catch trout." Holding her hand in a firm grip, he started for the falls again.

Shaking back her hair, Anya followed. She felt a little like a child again, wading through the tame, slow creek behind her father's house, where fat minnows had darted around her ankles. Except that now all her perceptions were sharpened: the sun so hot on her back, the water so cold, the air so pure.

And the *sounds*. In the woodland silence, the stream murmured and hissed along the banks, burbled around the rocks, made a symphony of splashes and trilling trickles as they neared the tiny falls. Here the trees grew close, branches drooping like a green canopy over the rocks and rushing water. The sun struck through to lay moving patterns of greenish-gold on the stream. And, all the while, she was conscious of a current of warmth running from the broad palm and long fingers that gripped her hand, exciting and somehow protective.

"Hold on," Brady whispered, swinging his arm back to stop her. "See that overhanging boulder on your right? Look beneath it, but don't move."

Anya looked, seeing nothing at first but the shadow of the rock and the dappled surface. Then, as she watched, a tail moved lazily, a shape took form. "I see him," she whispered back. "Is that his home?"

Brady grinned. "Maybe. He's resting." He raised his head and scanned the bank along the stream thoughtfully, then looked back at her. "I feel like showing off, so this probably won't work. But I'll try. Can you stand very still?"

She nodded, her green eyes sparkling. "Are you going to catch him?"

"I hope so. Don't move." He released her hand and stepped quietly back down the stream, then moved toward the bank and climbed up. Staying among the trees so his shadow wouldn't touch the water, he moved upstream and came back above the big rock. Anya watched him kneel and then stealthily flatten himself along the rock. Slowly, he extended a long arm downward until the tips of his fingers were in the water.

Anya's mouth curved in a gently derisive smile. If Brady thought he was going to grab that trout, he was in for a rude surprise. Even the tiniest minnow knew enough to dart away. She watched his hand, which appeared to be immobile, and then realized it wasn't. The tips of his fingers were now a good two inches below the surface, and she hadn't seen him move.

She concentrated and caught the almost imperceptible movement as the hand crept steadily downward, a fraction of an inch at a time. Then it was level with the wavering shape of the trout, and the fingers were slowly curling. She drew in her breath with amazement as she saw the tips of his fingers stroke along the underside of the fish, slow and lazy, in a curiously sensual motion. The trout lay still, only his gills moving in and out, and Brady's thumb began to edge nearer, circling...

"Got him!" A silver spray of water arced up, fanned out, and splattered Anya from knees to neck. Brady's hand was high in the air, holding the wildly struggling trout, its rainbow sides shining. "Fine and fat," he said triumphantly, "but not wise. He liked the stroking, but he'll be smarter the next time."

Anya was gasping, wiping the water from her arms, her eyes wide. "I wouldn't have believed it if I hadn't seen it," she said, laughing. "That was marvelous, Brady—fantastic! Is that the Indian way?"

"One of them." Brady had flattened himself on the rock again, lowering the trout to the water and submerging him gently. In minutes, the frightened flutter of gills slowed to normal, and Brady opened his hand. The fish shot away like a streak of dark lightning, heading downstream. Swinging himself around, Brady dropped back into the water and came to take Anya's hand. She smiled up at him, all the wariness gone from her green eyes.

"You didn't hurt him at all, Brady. That was kind."

He looked away, somehow embarrassed. "Don't make me out to be a saint," he said gruffly. "It would have ended differently if I had been hungry." He turned her back downstream. "We won't go any further—the water gets deeper near the falls. We'll stick to the shallows today."

With the water rushing ahead of them, the fine silt they disturbed clouded in front of them, making it difficult to see. Anya stumbled and Brady drew her closer, steadying her with an arm around her waist. When she stumbled again, distracted as much by the arm as the uncertain footing, Brady picked her up and carried her the short distance remaining. Collapsing on the blanket, he gave an exaggerated groan.

"You're slim but you're solid, lady. How much do you weigh?"

"A hundred and fifteen," Anya told him, shaving off two pounds without shame. She gave him a wicked grin. "Maybe you're out of shape." She was breathless herself, her whole body tingling and aware from the pressure of his arms, the feel of his chest, the scent of his warmth. They were both half lying on the blanket, and she moved away from him, leaning back on propped elbows and tilting her face to the sun. Now, if she could just keep this casual . . .

"This has been fun," she said, closing her eyes against the brightness, "even educational, with a lesson in fishing. But I'd better be going now . . ."

Brady was lying on his side, and she sensed his gaze surveying the shape of her breasts in the dampened, clinging shirt, the slender, bare legs with the rumpled skirt above the rounded knees. Her eyes slitted, she saw his gaze rise to her tangled hair and flushed face, the soft mouth still parted in a smile.

"Not yet," he said huskily. "I want to see if I was right."

Anya felt his arm slip beneath her propped shoulders. Her eyes flew open and stared into his, finding them intensely blue, the black pupils expanding. Her quick protest was muffled by his mouth, and her elbows slipped out from under her beneath the weight of his descending chest. In a split-second, she was flat on her back, half covered by his warmth, his scent in her nostrils and his tongue doing indescribably sensuous things to her mouth.

She panicked, her hands flying to his shoulders, pushing hard, her body twisting, trying to escape. She wrenched her face away, managing a broken sound. "Br-Brady . . ."

"Mmm-m-m," he breathed, curling over her to capture her mouth again, "even sweeter than I thought it would be." His tongue ran along the soft inner flesh of her lips, prodding them open again, slipped in, and possessed her mouth, thrusting gently and then thrusting again, a subtle promise of the ultimate bliss of mating.

Anya stilled, helpless, feeling her pounding heartbeat matched by his, hard against her breasts. One big hand had traveled under her skirt, wrapped itself around her silky thigh, the fingers kneading the soft flesh. She remembered her nakedness, open to his questing hand, and was suddenly suffused with a delicious warmth, a blind, sharp yearning that drove out every rational thought.

With a sound somewhere between a moan and a whimper, she yielded. Her tense muscles relaxed by themselves and melted against him; her hands stopped pushing and slipped to the back of his head, burying themselves in his thick hair. She felt weightless, soaring, her blood beating a tom-tom through her veins, clear to her fingertips, her toes. Beneath his chest, her breasts tightened, pushing hardened tips against him. Her tongue danced with his, softly urging.

Breaking off the kiss, breathing hard, Brady raised his head and looked down into half-closed, sultry green eyes, shining above a soft moist mouth waiting for more. His arms tightened, his body arched closer, and her loins turned to his like a sunflower to the sun. She was his right now, and they both knew it.

"Anya..."

Anya stared up at him in dazed surprise, hearing the tortured sound of warning in his voice. The eyes boring into hers were black with passion, with only a narrow blue rim around the dark pupils. The musky scent of arousal was drifting between them in the clear air, yet there was denial in his rugged face. Muscles rippled along a set jaw as he forced himself away from her and sat up, hunching over his knees.

"I'm sorry," he said flatly. "Too much too soon. Right?" He glanced around at the puzzled, hurt expression on her softened face and scooped her up savagely, holding her tight against his side. "Love, another second of that and I wouldn't have stopped. And somehow I don't think you're the kind that goes on a picnic with a stranger and ends up making love in the crumbs." He pushed the thick hair back from her flushed face and managed his grin. "Are you? We can always start over."

"I'm not," Anya said shakily, "but I would have been this time. Something happened . . ."

"*We* happened," Brady said, and pulled her closer, tucking her head under his chin, wrapping both arms around her. "Smokey the Bear will be after us for starting a fire in his forest. Umm-m-m, you smell so good, you feel so good, and you're so damned beautiful to me. I've got to have you, love, but not like this." He rocked her gently, bending to nuzzle his face in her hair, his fingers kneading her slender back, slipping around to cup a breast and brush the hard little nubbin with a thumb. Then he had let her go and was on his feet. "Damn!" he said feelingly, and walked away to the edge of the stream, standing there with his head bent, his rangy body tense, his hands in his pockets.

Anya had no difficulty understanding his problem. Her own body was screaming, *Why not? Why not?* She picked up her shoes and the crumpled handful of pantyhose and disappeared into the edge of the woods. When she came back, she was properly dressed and very subdued.

Brady had picked up every atom of debris; the bag was stuffed with empty beer cans and sandwich wrappings. Snapping the blanket in the air, he gave her a wry grin.

"I'll be darned if it isn't Mrs. Meredith, with her armor in place," he said, folding the blanket efficiently. "You can carry this." He pushed it into her arms and put a hand on each side of her head, tilting her face up. "End of Act One," he added softly. "Mad at me?"

"No," Anya said, "just confused. I wanted you very much." Her clear green eyes met his with utter candor. "I didn't want to stop, but I'm glad you did." She felt his long fingers tighten in her hair, saw his steady gaze deepen.

"Are you always that honest with a man?"

"Never."

"Then why with me?"

"Because you're a stranger, I suppose," Anya said thoughtfully. "You know—it's like telling your problems to a person on a ship or a train. You can be honest then, because when the trip is over, you'll never see him again."

His mouth was marked again by tenderness. "What if suddenly you end up in the same place, love? What, then?"

She looked at him uncertainly. "Why, I guess you'd hate each other for knowing too much, or, maybe you'd be very close."

"I'll settle for that," Brady said, and turned her toward the van.

Chapter 3

THE POSTON HOME was outside of town, set on the southern slope of a hill and overlooking a wooded ravine. It was rather isolated, since the land around it on three sides was part of the Chattahoochee National Forest, and the Postons had no neighbors. As usual, driving up the winding road from the highway that evening, Anya thought how lucky Marilee and Roger had been to find a place so ideal for their large family. Plenty of space for the children to romp, no neighbors to complain about the noise, and no traffic except for their own cars and an occasional visitor. Except, she noted with surprise, that tonight there was a police cruiser parked in front of the wide porch, a trooper leaning on the hood and a distracted-looking Marilee listening to what he had to say.

Anya's heart sank as, inevitably, she wondered what had happened. Pulling in behind the cruiser, thinking of the worst things first—an accident to Roger, a lost child, a thief in the house—she jumped out, her eyes on Marilee's face. Then Marilee gave her a careless grin. Relaxing, Anya walked over.

"It's nothing," Marilee said reassuringly. "Just a warning."

The trooper frowned. "Don't take it lightly, Mrs. Poston. The men are considered dangerous. You're advised to use every precaution." His eyes went over Anya with growing interest. He was youngish, perhaps in his mid-thirties, a well-built man in his uniform, with brown hair and eyes that matched. "This is your cousin who's visiting, Mrs. Poston?"

"Yes," Marilee answered. "Mrs. Meredith, Officer."

The interest in the brown eyes was replaced by a faint regret. "I see. Well, please tell her and your husband what I've told you, and be sure your doors are bolted securely and your windows locked. And, if you see anyone who looks suspicious . . ."

"I'll call," Marilee said patiently, "right away." She gave him a sudden grin. "We have five children and three dogs. A man would have to be crazy to break in here."

The brown eyes surveyed her coolly. "This kind likes hostages, ma'am. Take no chances." He nodded at Anya, then climbed back into the cruiser.

Anya shivered, going toward the house. "Hostages, good Lord! He meant to frighten us, didn't he? What is it—escaped convicts?"

Marilee shrugged. "Escaped suspects, not convicts. Two political prisoners who managed to get away from federal authorities before they were tried. But they were last seen a hundred miles north of here, so I think the police are just being super careful." She hesitated. "Except they seem to think there's some connection in Helen." Stopping on the wide porch, a covered area with old-fashioned rockers and baskets of ferns, she looked at Anya seriously. "Please don't mention it in front of the children. I don't want them frightened."

Anya nodded. "But why warn us? We don't live in Helen."

"Because of the forest," Marilee explained. "They say the men are foreign, but connected in some way with a renegade bunch of survivalists who wander the national forest. But there are millions of acres, and we're nowhere near the remote areas the survivalists like. Don't let it bother you, cuz." She came up with her usual sparkling smile and put her hand on the door. "Come on in here, where it's really dangerous."

Inside the big, high-ceilinged hall they were met by a mad rush of children and dogs, sending throw rugs sliding across the polished wood floor, yelling and yelping. Laughing, Anya picked up a small body that slid to a stop at her feet. Sara, she guessed, since the round face carried a bruise on the chin instead of the forehead. She hugged her, listening to the questions.

"Did he bring you a ticket, Mom? What did you do bad?"

"Are you 'rested? Do you have to go to jail?"

The three beagles circled the crowd, tails wagging, uttering excited, melodious yelps.

"Quiet!"

Marilee really had a tremendous voice for such a little woman. Effective, too. Silence fell, and into it she said calmly, "The officer was just being friendly, letting us know he's around if we need him. Now, all of you, get to your jobs or there won't be any dessert tonight. You're between me and the kitchen."

Miraculously, a path opened that led directly to the back of the hall. Marilee picked up the other twin and marched through, followed by Anya. Turning at the door of the kitchen, Marilee fixed her eyes on the tallest child first. "Rog, you have homework. Becky, I want you to sort the laundry. Steven, you're in charge of feeding the dogs. Okay?"

Three heads nodded, and three voices chorused, "Okay!"

"How do you do it?" Anya marveled, closing the kitchen door and plunking Sara in a high chair. "I'd never manage."

"Sure you would," Marilee said, putting Susan in the other chair. "It comes with the package." She glanced at the clock and turned to the stove. "Roger will be home in an hour. He's showing property on the other side of the county. I'll get the kids fed and settled, and when he's here we'll talk over what we're supposed to do."

Helping Marilee give the twins an early meal, and setting places for the other children, Anya realized that beneath her calm exterior Marilee was tight with tension. She wasn't as casual about the trooper's warning as she had pretended. Inside the warm, old-fashioned, and homey house, it all seemed unreal. Looking around at the ruffled country curtains, the sturdy furniture, and homespun rugs, it was impossible to imagine some desperate man holding this family hostage. But if there was one bright spot in the situation, it was the fact that this new topic for thought was holding her own tangled emotions at bay, giving her time to recover a little before she started untangling them. And the trooper's warning had occupied Marilee's usually probing mind and kept her from asking where Anya had been all afternoon.

Anya would have been more comfortable if it hadn't been for Brady's parting words.

"You're going to see a lot of me," he'd said, helping her out of the van in the parking lot where her own car was parked. "I refuse to be a stranger on a train or ship. And don't try to hide. I know where the Postons live."

By then, Anya had been finding it hard to believe how uninhibited she had been with this—this stranger. Because he *was* a stranger, no matter what he and her idiotic body kept telling her. She had looked away, wondering how to answer him.

"I won't be here long," she'd said finally, "not long enough for us to get to know each other well." She had edged toward her car, embarrassed again when she remembered how close they had come to knowing each other in the biblical sense.

"Don't run out on me," Brady had said gently, and reached past her to open her car door. His chest brushing against her shoulder had made her dizzy with longing. Settled in the seat, she had felt suddenly deprived.

"I'm not exactly running out on you," she had said shortly. "I had already planned to leave on Monday."

Leaning on her window, Brady had grinned. "We'll concentrate on you getting to know me. I feel as if I have known you all my life."

She had looked at the bending line of his lean, virile body and remembered how it had felt, pinning her down on that blanket. "I'd better go," she had said faintly.

"Marilee will be worrying about me."

Driving away, she had been perversely glad that Brady hadn't known her all her life. Tom Meredith had known her all her life and had found her inadequate. She had clutched the steering wheel tightly, thinking of that. Maybe any man who knew her well would feel the same. Maybe, inside, she was nothing. Even boring. If so, she didn't want Brady Durant to find it out.

By the time Marilee had chased the children off to bed, Roger Poston was home. He breezed into the kitchen, kissed Marilee soundly, and ruffled Anya's hair on the way to the refrigerator. Of medium height and squarely built, Roger was as blond as Marilee was dark, as broad as she was thin, but their energy and good humor matched perfectly. He took a bottle of beer from the refrigerator, snapped off the cap, and sat down on a stool, staring at his wife.

"Let's have it," he said. "I know it's coming. One of the kids sick?"

"No." Marilee gave Anya a wry smile. "He always knows when I'm worried, no matter how I try to hide it." She opened the oven and brought out a casserole, holding it carefully with two thick pads. Placing it on the kitchen table, she sighed and straightened, rubbing the small of her back. "Let's eat out here. I don't think I can make it to the dining room."

Anya leaped to bring mats and silverware, while Roger got up and began massaging Marilee's shoulders. "That bad, huh? Tell me about it, baby."

"Oh, it's nothing," Marilee said, elaborately casual, "just a couple of terrorists, running around in our forest."

Roger's hands stilled on her shoulders and turned her to face him. *"Terrorists?* What in hell are you talking about?"

Marilee's laugh was on the ragged edge of hysteria. "Not really terrorists, Roger. At least, I hope not. But the police want us all locked up and staying inside until they catch two escaped foreigners they think are dangerous. If Betty Sue hears it, I'll be out of a baby-sitter

again." Her mouth quivering, she leaned forward and
put her forehead against his shoulder. "I'm *scared*, hon.
That damned trooper said these men would—would like
hostages. I keep thinking of the kids."

Silently laying down mats and plates, distributing
silverware, Anya thought how courageous Marilee was
when she was in charge of house and children, and how
when Roger came home his strength allowed her to let
out her fears, open up and release her feelings. Roger
was pressing Marilee down into a chair, murmuring
reassurances, bringing her a glass of wine.

"Drink it," he commanded, and poured one for Anya.
"You, too, cuz. I haven't seen a smile since I came in.
It can't be that bad." He seated Anya, brought the salad
from the refrigerator, got out the homemade bread and
cutting board, and sat down with an exaggerated sigh.
"A man's work is never done," he complained, and
grinned, though there wasn't much humor in his steady
gray eyes. "Now, baby, give it to me from the beginning."

Relaxing, sipping her wine, Marilee went through
it, ending with the fact that the police thought the two
escapees had joined a group of survivalists. Roger
looked disbelieving.

"Where are these two 'political' prisoners supposed
to be from?"

Marilee shrugged. "The trooper didn't know. All he
said was that they were in the country illegally."

Roger laughed, relieved. "Anything from scared Mex-
ican wetbacks to Haitians could qualify. After a week or
two of living with survivalists, they'll be glad to give
themselves up and go home."

Anya was suddenly curious. "I thought survivalists
were just people who go out in the woods for weekends
and practice living off the land." She laughed uncertainly.
"Preparing for doomsday."

"Some are," Roger agreed, "but some aren't. There
are all kinds. Roving, heavily armed bands of fanatics
and misfits claim the survivalist tag so they'll be let alone.
But I haven't heard of any like that around here." He

patted Marilee's arm. "I suggest you satisfy the trooper by keeping the kids close to the house, tell Betty Sue to report any strangers she sees, and we'll lock up tight in the evenings. The police will be checking, so let's cooperate." He poured another glass of wine for them both, got himself another beer, and sat down. "Now, what's in that casserole that smells so darned good?"

Anya's bedroom was on the third floor of the old house, the windows facing the wooded ravine below. That night she sat for a time on the deep windowsill and looked out over the moon-silvered forest. The shadowy depths she had thought so innocently pretty before now seemed, like the depths of her newly discovered emotions, wild and mysterious, holding and hiding something dangerous. She shivered, thinking of Brady's plundering mouth on hers, and the wild, uncontrollable way her body had responded. For thirty-one years that body had done what her mind had told it to do, but now . . . She shifted restlessly as desire spread its beguiling heat deep in her belly. She still wanted him. Brady had ended that lovemaking, she hadn't. He had had her, and then let her go.

Like the trout, she thought suddenly. The trout had liked his stroking and let itself be captured, and so had she. She laughed ruefully and stood up, taking off her warm robe and slipping into bed. She had gotten away, and the sooner she left here and settled into a job in New York, the better. A man with that kind of magic could tear a woman's heart out.

"I hate to ask you," Marilee said at breakfast, "but could you stay on until they catch those men? Then I could be here in the mornings, and Roger plans to drop by every afternoon. I'd feel safer, and so will Betty Sue. I'm afraid she'll quit. She's nervous out here anyway."

There was no way to refuse. No matter what Roger had said about harmless refugees, the fact remained that the trooper had said the men were dangerous. Anya sighed inwardly and brought out a smile.

"Of course I'll stay. No one in New York is holding his breath waiting for me to report to work." She finished her coffee and stood up. "I'll get dressed and go open up the shop."

Marilee laughed, surprised. "On Sunday? Only Roger works on Sunday—he's out showing a house."

Anya blinked. She had always prided herself on her logic and efficiency, and now she didn't even know what day it was. "I see why you want me to stay," she said wryly. "Where else could you find such an alert, with-it saleslady? Okay, I've got a day off. I'll wash my hair, my clothes, my car..." She wandered off, making her way through a knot of children, dogs, coloring books, and crayons sprawled in the hall. Thank heaven for the coloring books. Last week the kids had made murals on the living room wall.

Anya was crouched on the back steps brushing her hair dry in the sunshine when she heard the low-pitched whine and steady chipping sound of a diesel engine coming up the incline from the highway. She drew in a deep breath, feeling her body contracting, her skin suddenly sensitive under the jeans and the loose-knit sweater she was wearing. She wasn't surprised. She had been half listening for the van, aware that in some part of herself she was hoping to hear it, though her reason was violently against it. She went on brushing the silky, nearly dry strands, telling herself she should have told Marilee what had happened, and told her, too, that she didn't want to see Brady again. But she couldn't, even now, imagine telling anyone what a fool she had been.

Tensely, she listened to Brady's decisive footsteps on the porch, the imperative knock. Then the sound of Marilee's tapping heels, the burst of surprised welcome at the door.

"Why, yes, she's here." Marilee's clear voice, pleased. "Come in. I'll find her for you." Sounds of movement, Brady's deep voice, the shutting door.

Conquering a wild impulse to leap up, run around the corner of the house, and hide, Anya stood up on shaking legs, tossed back her mass of shining hair, and turned reluctantly as Marilee's bright face poked out the back door.

"Brady Durant is here," Marilee said, sotto voce. "Why didn't you tell me he was coming?" She came out, shutting the door, and stared uncertainly at Anya's wide, defenseless green eyes. "When did you see him again? He didn't come into the shop yesterday."

Anya dropped her gaze to the hairbrush in her hand. "We—met on the street. And—well, I wasn't sure he'd be here today." She glanced up, forcing a smile. "You know—it was one of those vague plans people make . . ."

"Humph!" Marilee's brown eyes narrowed. "Brady's about the least vague person I know. Anyway, he's here, and you'd better go rescue him before he's inundated with kids. My children, unfortunately, love strangers." She swept over Anya with a glance as she turned and opened the door again. "Unless you'd like to skip up the back stairs and fix yourself up a bit?"

Anya shook her head. What difference did it make how she looked? The worse the better, maybe. She gathered her courage and strode ahead of Marilee, her bare feet cool on the polished wood floor, her loose sweater flapping, her hair a wild cloud around her pale face. She wheeled smartly at the open door of the living room and saw Brady sitting in Roger's big chair, covered with children. Becky, Steven, and Sara were all on his lap; Roger, Jr., was leaning on his shoulder; and Susan, a thumb in her mouth and a crayon in her hand, had her back to him. She was beginning another mural. Long, masterful strokes of brilliant red swept across the wall. Hardly worth stopping her now. Brady looked up and grinned at her.

"Room for one more," he said cheerfully, and patted his knee.

It was just as Anya had thought it would be. One look at that grin and she melted. Her insides ran together warmly; a smile took over her mouth. He had to be the most dangerous man she had ever met. Well, she could

at least *try* to keep it light. She went in and perched
gingerly on the offered knee, listening to the racket as
the kids competed for his attention. They were showing
him their coloring books and insisting that he judge which
was best. Anya watched him industriously turning pages,
poring over the wild colors. The black brows were knitted, the thick black lashes shadowing his blue eyes. Such
luxurious lashes, she thought, ridiculous on the rough,
creased face.

"This one," he said suddenly, holding it up. "I like
this one the best."

"That's Susan's," Becky said disdainfully. "The twin
over there painting the wall. She can't even stay in the
lines."

"That's why I like it," Brady said seriously. "I can't,
either."

Marilee had clearly been eavesdropping. She swept
into the room, grabbed the red crayon from Susan's hand,
and smacked her bottom. Carrying the indignantly
screaming child out, she turned at the door and looked
at the others.

"Mr. Durant came to see Annie Anya," she said with
meaning. "Mind your manners."

Children fell from Brady's lap like a waterfall and
flowed out the door after their mother, shutting it carefully behind them. Brady gathered the scatter of crumpled
pages from his neat brown gabardine slacks and looked
at Anya, still perched stiffly on his knee.

"Annie Anya?" His voice was soft, intimate, teasing.

Anya jumped up, taking the coloring books from him,
putting them on a table. "Some of them can't pronounce
Auntie," she said shortly. She was embarrassed now by
her appearance. Brady looked wonderful. The gabardine
slacks were set off by a silky white shirt; a matching
jacket hung over the back of the chair. And here she
was, slopping around in bare feet and jeans, this awful
sweater.

"Go change," Brady said pleasantly, giving her a weird
feeling of being transparent. "We're going to Atlanta."

Anya whirled and stared at him. "I can't. I—well, it's too *far*. And, besides, I don't like cities."

"It's not far, and we won't be inside the city." Brady stood up, clasped her shoulders, and drew her close, a movement so smooth and quick it gave her no time to move away. She put her hands against his chest to keep distance between them, but somehow the silky feel of his shirt and the hard warmth beneath it coaxed the hands around to his back. Thick muscles rippled under her palms as he bent to kiss her.

"No."

"Yes." He caught her mouth with his, and when she twisted to free herself, she found his hand embedded in her flyaway hair, holding. She was still, gasping under the sensuous magic of his firm mouth. Warmth flowed through her in an irresistible tide. Her lips opened to him; her slim arms tightened around his bulk. Then they were both moving, fitting the hard planes of his body against the soft curves of hers, swaying. Under the loose sweater, her breasts were deliciously crushed by the pressure of his chest. She drew in a breath, and the breath was his; the very essence of him filled her mouth and throat. It held his scent, his taste, and something more—a kind of knowing that this was her place, that all that mattered was the way their mouths knew how to caress each other, the way their bodies knew how to fit and mingle their warmth. The feel of his hands moving on her back was heavenly.

"Oh! Excuse me..."

Anya hadn't heard the door open, but she heard it close after the surprised grunt and apology. She jerked away, her already flushed face turning pinker.

"Roger came home," she whispered. "He—he saw us."

"So he did," Brady said in a normal tone, though he looked dazed. "Who cares?" He tried to pull her back into his arms, but she stepped away.

"I'll change," she said in a quick reversal of attitude. "I won't be a minute." She fled, practically running from the room and up the stairs. With any luck, she could throw on something and be out of the house before Roger told what he had seen and aroused Marilee's insatiable curiosity.

She was putting on the only outfit she had that would suit the occasion—a green silk suit with an unstructured loose jacket and a cunningly draped and slitted skirt that showed off her long legs—when Marilee slipped in. Marilee wore a look of amazement and carried a hanger holding a cream-colored silk blouse with a ripple of collar outlining a deep V neck. She thrust it toward Anya.

"I knew what you'd be wearing," she said, "and you're not going to ruin it with one of those Mother Hubbard shirts of yours."

Applying lip gloss, Anya refused even to look. "This will be fine," she said, indicating the tailored blouse she had on. "I haven't time to—"

"Either you wear it, or I go down and ask Brady just what's been going on between you two," Marilee said firmly. "I may even ask him what his intentions are."

With a frustrated groan, Anya threw off the jacket and began unbuttoning her shirt. "It isn't *anything,*" she hissed, strangled, and grabbed the blouse from the hanger. "You know very well how casual everyone is these days about—about relationships." She pulled the blouse over her head and stuffed the tails into the top of her skirt, groaning again at the sight of all the exposed cleavage. The deep V plunged past the swelling sides of her high breasts, and the rippling collar only called attention to them. "This isn't right for me, Marilee!"

"Wear your dark green heels," Marilee said, unperturbed. "Will you be back tonight?"

Anya threw her a wild glance. "Of course! For heaven's sake! What did you think?"

Marilee grinned. "I could say I thought you were having a—er, casual relationship. But, knowing you, I won't."

Drawing a deep breath, Anya picked up the hairbrush again to bring some kind of order to the thick mass of stubborn hair. There was just no answer to that.

The men were having a beer on the front porch when Anya and Marilee came down. Roger was expounding on property values and real-estate taxes, and Brady was listening politely. He stood up with barely concealed relief when Anya appeared, told the Postons good-bye, also politely, and hurried her toward the van.

"Wait!" Roger came striding after them, and for an agonized minute Anya thought he might be about to come on as a protective male and would ask all those things her father used to ask when she went on a date. But he merely held out a key.

"You'll need it," he said. And he added to Brady, "We usually don't lock up after dark out here in the boon-docks, but with those prisoners at large, we're cooper-ating with the police."

"I heard about that," Brady said slowly, and swept the forest around them with a thoughtful gaze. "Good idea. It's a vulnerable area."

So am I, Anya thought, tucking the key into her purse and climbing into the van. A very vulnerable area. Only, unlike the forest, she had created her own terrorists to hold her hostage. This wild desire to be with a perfect stranger was definitely foreign to her, and certainly ter-rorizing. She glanced at Brady as he climbed in beside her and remembered that she had planned to tell him she wouldn't see him again. Well, she could tell him now that this was the last time. She opened her mouth, hes-itated, and then shut it again as the engine started and the van rolled forward. Somehow the words just wouldn't come out.

Chapter 4

"WE'RE GOING TO a small town," Brady said, turning from the Postons' private road onto the highway, "just outside Atlanta. There's a regional art show going on there, and I thought you might like to see it."

Anya glanced at him warily. It was the first time either of them had spoken since they had gotten into the van. Brady seemed as tense as she felt. His hands were tight on the steering wheel, his body seemed taut all over, and his black brows were still drawn together. But she could feel the pull of his magnetism all the same. Her fingers wanted to smooth the frown, massage the tightness from the wide shoulders. Maybe massage him all over. She looked away, conscious of her beating heart, the tremble in her stomach.

"I like art shows," she said, making an effort to sound politely agreeable. "Are you exhibiting in it?"

He shook his head. "I wanted the trip, that's all." They had come to a long, rolling stretch of road like a big roller coaster ahead of them. He settled back in the seat and looked over with a trace of his grin. "So we could be alone with my hands occupied. Otherwise, how could I tell you the story of my life?" He wiggled his thick brows at her with a comical leer. "With my hands free, I'd be busy investigating the curves I see peeking at me from that sexy blouse."

Anya pulled her loose jacket tighter. "It's Marilee's blouse," she said crossly, "and it isn't the curves that are doing the peeking. Tell me the story of your life."

"I was a foundling," Brady said dramatically. "It has long been suspected that I have royal blood in my veins . . ." He gave her a haughty look, his brows raised. "You aren't buying that? I don't look the part? Well, then, I'll tell you I'm thirty-seven years old and considered reasonably normal by my friends. I make a scanty living by painting, nicely supplemented by a trust fund left to me by my parents. And," he added, his smile fading, "I've been married. A long time ago. A long, dreary time ago." He was staring at the road again. "I hope none of that makes a difference to you."

"How could it?" Anya's voice was strained. "It's quite a lot like mine, given a difference of six years." She was telling herself angrily not to be ridiculous. Of course he would have been married, been in love. A man that attractive, that age. She should have known. She stared out into the woodlands, deeply jealous of a woman she didn't know, a woman who had once lain in his arms. "Why are you telling me this, anyway?"

"So I won't be a stranger," Brady said, his grin coming back. "Are you beginning to know me? A wastrel, living mostly on inherited money, playing with paint in the mountains. A totally irresponsible wanderer—who happens to be crazy about you."

Anya twisted in the seat, her green eyes startled. "Are you? Crazy about me, I mean?"

"God, *yes,*" Brady said feelingly, and reached for her hand, gripping it hard. "You hit me like a ton of bricks, Annie Anya. I feel like a—a kid." He slowed the suddenly wavering van and then awkwardly bumped off the pavement, rolling into the graveled entrance to a farm road, plowing along until they stopped at a barred and locked gate. Cars whizzed past on the highway behind them as they sat staring into each other's eyes. "Couldn't you tell?" Brady asked hoarsely, still gripping her hand. "Or have you just been trying to tell me to get lost?"

Anya's eyes misted, and her heart bounced wildly. "Not—not exactly. I'm not leaving as soon as I thought . . . " What was she saying? That they had time for a short affair? She drew in a deep breath. "Listen," she added awkwardly. "I'm crazy about you, too. But I'm n-not very interesting once you get to know me."

Brady looked at her incredulously, reached across the wide space between them, and pulled her into an awkward embrace. "You interest me," he said huskily, "to the point of complete distraction. Damn these bucket seats!"

In spite of the seats, the kiss was long and very satisfactory. Honking horns and raucous cheering from passing cars finally broke them apart.

"Then it's settled?" Brady's blue gaze was a sky full of stars to Anya. "We're crazy about each other?"

Anya laughed shakily and collapsed back into her seat. "That sounds like an accurate description." Crazy was right. Her heart was pounding so hard she could hear it, feel it thumping in her skin. It was true. They were crazy about each other, and the thought was both marvelous and terrifying. Because there was only one logical conclusion to the way they felt. That short affair would happen, and she wasn't the kind for a short affair. She glanced at him as he settled into his seat and started the engine. Maybe, just this once . . .

The diesel roared, and the big van swung back and shot gravel behind it as it roared onto the highway again. Brady shifted gears with a fine carelessness, giving her a warmly possessive look that took her breath away. Then he speeded up, his eyes on the road. He was humming, a deep, throaty sound almost inaudible amid the noise of engine and wind. Curled in the seat, with cool air blowing on her cheeks, Anya only half listened. It didn't matter what he was humming; he was happy. She was happy. She was only fearful when she thought of the future, so she didn't.

Reaching the small town of Brooksville, they wound their way through to find the signs and flying banners of the Hungry Artists' Fall Show. They had to park blocks away, walking back to the community center through lazy, leaf-strewn streets that reminded Anya of the town where she had always lived. The thought was no longer bitter; that life seemed far away.

There was a carnival air around the large building of the center, with concession stands and open-air exhibits lining the wide pathways that led toward the doors.

"Dignified, it isn't," Brady commented. "You won't be reminded of the Louvre." With his arm around Anya's waist, he guided her through a jostling crowd and arrived unerringly at a stand selling sandwiches and coffee. "Roast beef or chicken?" he breathed in her ear. "Coffee or tea?"

"Either. Anything." Anya hadn't known she was hungry until she smelled the food, and she almost forgot it when his breath fanned her ear. After being served, they wandered on, munching, stopping to look at displays of stained glass, pottery, and hand-cut crystal.

"It's more like a fair," Anya said, leaving an exhibit of fossilized coral. "Where are the paintings?"

"Mostly inside." Brady stopped to stare at a tortured mass of black metal taller than he was. "What's that?"

Anya chuckled. "You're the artist. You tell me." She leaned and peered at the nameplate. "It's called Time Bomb."

Brady led her toward the building. "We don't need a potentially explosive item. We *are* one."

Anya believed him, once they were in the narrow, long hall that led to the main exhibition room. It was packed with shuffling bodies, two serpentine lines going in opposite directions. Poked and pushed from every direction, she was conscious only of Brady's warm side and the hand that had originally been resting on her waist. He was taking advantage of the pressing, oblivious crowd and the slow pace. The hand was exploring beneath her loose jacket, moving warmly over the silky blouse to the soft undercurve of a breast. A light dew of perspiration appeared on Anya's upper lip. She glanced up and found Brady's blue eyes studying her plunging neckline.

"Animal!" Her whisper came out with a gasp. "You're crazy."

A thumb brushed across the breast gently, and his eyes

met hers with warm seductiveness. "I thought we'd agreed on that."

"I'll scream," she whispered, and saw his grin flash. "You wouldn't."

No, she wouldn't. But there had to be some way to stop this teasing before she exploded. Some *revenge* ... she moved slightly ahead, bringing her rounded buttock into firm contact with his loins. The swaying shuffle of the tightly packed crowd was ideal. She let her hips stroke back and forth caressingly, applying a subtle pressure. In a few moments, his hand slipped down to her waist again and pulled her back to his side. She noted his flushed face with amusement.

"If you can't stand the heat, don't start the fire," she murmured, and he laughed.

"The result of that gambit would have been entirely too apparent." He had lowered his mouth to her ear, which was almost as arousing as his hand had been. Especially when he added softly, "I can hardly wait."

Anya smiled. They were coming to the end of the hall—she could see the big room ahead and the crowd dispersing in front of them. She had never felt so free, so intimate, with anyone before. So sure of what she wanted. Never with Tom. Fear touched her lightly, making her lower lip quiver. It would be terrible, leaving Brady ...

In the main exhibition room, there was order. Paintings were hung and lighted properly. There was nothing in the center of the space but two or three large sculptures, leaving room for the crowd to move freely. Taking her hand, Brady began a slow circuit of the walls.

"Hmm-m, Jensen is improving," he said, stopping in front of a large group of portraits, all of the Cherokee Indians. "Look at the character in that face."

Anya looked. But when Brady continued to study the detail in the portraits, she began to look at the people around them. Some faces were rapt and wondering, others bored. She wondered if the artists themselves mingled, listening for comments. Then a woman caught her eye, a truly beautiful woman with pale gold hair and violet-blue eyes, dressed in an amazing outfit that had evidently been made of silk scarves. Brilliant color swathed her small, perfect figure; points of the scarves were draped around bare legs adorned with gold ankle chains and jeweled sandals. An artist or an entertainer? She was about to ask Brady when the woman faced their way.

"Brady!" The woman came half running, her ankle chains sliding, scarves flying, while beside her Anya felt Brady stiffen and turn.

"Hello, Morgan," he said flatly as the woman arrived, and put out his hand. "How are—"

The rest of his greeting was lost as the woman ignored the hand and pulled his head down to kiss him thoroughly. She laughed up at him as he straightened. "I'm not your mother-in-law, Brady! Don't greet me like one! How are you, darling?"

"Fine." Frowning, Brady reached for Anya. "Anya, this is Morgan Whitcomb, my sister-in-law. Anya Meredith, Morgan. Now, tell me, what in hell are you doing at a regional art show? As I remember, you always said they were tacky."

"Ah, but that was before I had anything to show," Morgan said, laughing again. "I'm showing my collection, darling—hoping to sell or trade for something different. But you must see it! I've included that lovely music box you found for me. And, by the way, I'll have Whit write you a check for it. He's guarding the collection while I cruise around." She turned to Anya with a bright smile. "Brady found the loveliest treasure for me."

"Only after you told me where it was and insisted I buy it for you," Brady growled, but then smiled and tightened an arm around Anya. "Not that I object. That's where I found Anya. She sold it to me."

Morgan froze. Her violet-blue eyes turned slowly to Anya with a look of shock. "You own Postons' Art and Antiques?"

"Oh, no." Puzzled, Anya wondered why Morgan cared.

"The Postons are relatives. I've been helping out during a visit."

"How long have you been there?" Morgan flushed and added quickly, "Not that it matters, of course. Do you . . . uh . . . like Helen? I mean, are you planning on staying?"

Somehow, Anya got the impression that the last two questions were simply an effort to make the conversation seem like small talk, not important. What Morgan really wanted to know was how long she had been there. Now, why? Perversely, she answered only the last two.

"It's a nice place to visit, but I wouldn't want to live there."

"I see." Morgan looked wary. "Well, I won't keep you two. I imagine you have plans." She was turning away. "I'd better get back to my corner. Whit doesn't know a thing about selling or trading."

"About that check," Brady said pleasantly.

"Oh, you'll get it, darling. I'll send it to you tomorrow. Don't worry about it."

"I won't," Brady said, still pleasant. "We'll follow you over and get it now. Where Whit is, money is, right?"

Morgan tossed her head. "Whit won't mind. He knows it was worth it."

Walking across the big room, Anya couldn't help but notice how Morgan's undeniable beauty drew everyone's eyes. She didn't really need the costume and jewelry to attract attention. It had already occurred to Anya that since Morgan's last name wasn't Durant, she hadn't married into Brady's family. Brady had married into hers. So Morgan must be Brady's ex-wife's sister. Was his ex-wife also that beautiful?

Ahead of them now she could see the corner where a display of antique silver covered heavy glass shelves. A large and varied display, cleverly lighted. A tall man rose from a chair beside it and came to shake Brady's hand, smiling.

Anya concealed surprise as she was introduced to Paul

Whitcomb. Pleasant and assured, he was well past middle age, with a shock of white hair and deepset, kindly eyes in a wrinkled face. Twenty to twenty-five years between Morgan and her husband, Anya guessed, as well as a distinct difference in style. Whit looked extremely conventional.

"Darling," Morgan said sweetly, "will you write out a check for Brady? You know, for my lovely music box?"

"Certainly." The deepset eyes gleamed. "I had it appraised, Brady, and it's worth far more than you paid. I'm still surprised at you, finding something so valuable in that little tourist trap." Searching in the inside pocket of his coat for his checkbook, Whit missed the look that passed between Brady and Morgan. Then Brady shrugged and looked away.

"Come look at the collection while Whit takes care of that," Morgan said quickly, and drew them both toward the shelves. "Thanks for not giving away my little secret," she whispered breathlessly. "Sometimes, it's wise not to tell a husband everything." She raised her voice to a normal tone, and added, "See? I've given top billing to Jacob Bruner's masterpiece."

Grandly alone on the top shelf, the silver music box had its own small light placed to bring out the deep and elaborate carving. The top stood open, revealing the red velvet interior, richly shadowed. The light also illuminated the card propped beside it, which read: NOT FOR SALE OR TRADE.

"Why display it?" Brady asked coldly. "Pride of ownership, Morgan?"

Morgan's gaze flickered. "Why, no. It's just that there's been so much thievery lately—I like having it with me."

Whit laughed, coming up behind them. "That's true, Brady. She never leaves it at home—carries it in her bag, if you can believe that." He looked at Morgan with fond indulgence. "A favorite toy, isn't it, sweetheart?"

Anya, busy looking at the other shelves, was impressed by the variety. Silver tea sets, platters, plates, dozens of napkin rings, odd serving pieces of silverware. All with the deep glow of sterling. But not all antiques. Morgan wasn't above mixing in a few modern pieces of antique design. Not a serious collector, apparently. She turned back to the rest of them as Brady spoke to her. He was pocketing a check and holding out his hand.

"Ready to go, Anya?" His hand closed tightly over hers. "I think we've seen enough, haven't we?"

They had barely begun to look at the exhibits. But it took only a glance to see that Brady wanted to leave, now.

"Of course." She nodded politely at Morgan and Whit. "Glad to have met you. The display is beautiful..." Brady was walking away, taking her with him. "Goodbye," Anya called over her shoulder. "I hope I'll see you again."

"I hope you won't," Brady muttered savagely. "I can't stand being around that woman."

Anya waited until they had maneuvered through the crowded hall and were stepping outside into the chilly air. "Whatever else she may be," she said, her mind still on Brady's sister-in-law, "you'll have to admit she's still friendly to you. That's unusual, after a divorce. The in-laws usually—"

"I should have told you," Brady interrupted harshly, "we weren't divorced. My wife, Elisha, was killed in a car accident." He was taking her rapidly down the walk, his face twisted and pale, staring straight ahead. "She and Morgan were identical twins, and very close. I can't look at Morgan without seeing Elisha."

The shock of his words sent a deep shuddering sensation through Anya, breathlessly trying to keep up with him. "Oh, God," she said faintly, "I'm so sorry. I shouldn't have taken it for granted..."

Brady pulled her against his side with a savage gesture. "It's all in the past, love. If Morgan would leave me alone, it could stay there. I'm a fool to let her upset me after ten years." He hurried her along the street, shadowed now in the late-afternoon sun. Anya could feel the tension in his lean body, see pain in his taut face. Her chest felt leaden as she visualized Elisha. A young and fresh Morgan, a laughing ghost who still lived in Brady's memory. Half running now, shivering in the cold air, Anya thought how horrible it would be always to be reminded of what he had lost.

In the van, Brady closed off the back and turned on the heater, creating a warm cubicle around them. He seemed more relaxed, the lines in his face softening as he looked at her. "May as well enjoy the luxuries," he said, and switched on the stereo. Soft music poured around them as he reached and fastened a safety belt around Anya. "We're cutting out," he said, and smiled at her. "I'm not letting Morgan spoil our day. We'll stop for a good dinner on the way home and forget this mistake."

If he wanted to forget, she wanted to help him. She smiled back, kicked off her high heels, and tucked her legs up under her. "Let's go," she said. "It's forgotten."

But, of course, it wasn't. When they had finished their dinner at a local inn and strolled outside, Anya's mental image of Brady's lost love came back with smashing force. He had turned to her, his black hair shining under the yellow glow of the light in the lot, his dark face shadowed, his hand holding hers warmly.

"I'd like to stay," he said quietly. "Would you?"

A young and beautiful face, very like Morgan's, had seemed to float in the twilight between them. Who could compete with a ghost? Anya had turned away, hesitating, and felt his hand drop from hers.

"It's all right," he said evenly. "I said we'd give it time. Come on, I'll take you home."

At the Poston home, they had to use the key. The house was locked up tightly. Glancing behind them at the ravine below, the dark forest on either side, Anya thought of the trooper's warning and was glad Brady was with her. Coming into the dark hall, they were surprised by the glow of the kitchen light shining in the rear.

"Is that you, Anya?" Marilee appeared in the kitchen doorway in a robe and slippers. "Oh, and Brady! Good! Come back and have coffee with us. You'll never believe what has happened."

Sitting at the kitchen table, Marilee spun out her tale dramatically. "We were ready for bed when someone knocked on the door. I was afraid to open it, but Roger insisted that criminals don't knock, and *he* opened it. So, here were these two men, very well dressed, apologizing for the hour but saying they had an urgent reason." She paused, her thin face bright and excited, and looked at Roger.

"Do you want to tell them?"

Roger's gray eyes shone with tolerant amusement. "You're doing fine, hon."

"Well, they wanted the Bruner box!" Marilee burst out. "Can you imagine? After we gave up and cut the price in half! I asked if they were collectors, and they said they were agents for one, and Brady, I do believe you can make a nice profit if you want to sell. They said they'd pay the appraised price."

Brady leaned back and laughed wryly. "Now I feel bad for having paid what I thought was an exorbitant price for that thing. Sorry you missed the profit, Marilee. But I bought it for a collector, and she's paid for it. I doubt if she'll sell, but you can tell them I'll call her and give her the information."

Anya winced. One more time he would have to contact Morgan. But it couldn't be helped. "Odd," she said finally, "that the men couldn't wait until morning. I wonder how they found your house."

"I asked them that," Roger volunteered. "They said a state trooper gave them directions." He grinned. "I figured they must be honest. And they must work for a wealthy man. How many collectors can afford to hire agents to find their collectibles?"

"Someone must have carried the news," Anya said, laughing. "Or do you suppose it's the same man who wrote to you, Marilee? The one who ordered it?"

Marilee shook her head. "It wasn't him. They wouldn't tell me the name of the man they work for, but they did say it wasn't Morgan Whitcomb."

Anya's eyes shot to Brady's face and saw the same shock she felt. A shock that hardened into steely anger. He glanced at her and rose. "I'd better be going," he said with an attempt at casualness. "See me to the door, Anya?"

She followed him out into the dark hall and then onto the porch, almost afraid of the anger she could sense in his big body. He turned to her but kept a distance between them.

"She *used* me," he said violently, "and, damn her, it's the last time. She'll pay the price she agreed to pay when she ordered it, or I'll take the box back and bring it to the Postons' shop. Did you know she ordered it, Anya?"

"No, and I would never have suspected it. Marilee said it was a man, and she never mentioned the name until tonight. But, Brady, Morgan didn't know the price had been lowered . . ."

"She knew what she was supposed to pay," Brady said contemptuously, "and she could have told me. Either she plays fair for once in her life, or I'll tell Whit some of her background she doesn't want him to know. She learned these tricks from a gang of thieves and cheats she used to run with before she met Whit—hell, maybe she still does! But I'm not going to let her gyp the Postons."

Anya stared at him. "Why would a woman like Morgan be mixed up with thieves and cheats?"

"You don't know Morgan," Brady said, "and I wish I didn't. She has a taste for scum." His face was a mask of anger as he swung away and then hesitated at the top of the steps. Turning back, he caught Anya in a close embrace and stood there, holding her, for a long moment. "Please," he said finally, his deep voice strained, "don't blame me for losing my temper. She's ruined the best day I've had for years—a day with you, Annie Anya."

Her arms had slipped around him naturally, and her head had found the hollow of his neck and shoulder. She nuzzled the firm flesh beneath his ear. "There will be more days," she murmured, intoxicated all over again by the feel of his skin, by his scent. At this moment, she bitterly regretted her hesitation in the parking lot of the inn.

"But I can't spare any days," Brady whispered. "I want them all. I'm greedy for you, darling."

Anya kissed him, her soft mouth tentative but desirous, finding his in the dark. Brady reacted with a deep sound, crushing her closer, taking the offered mouth with a fierce tenderness. His hands moved over her back as if memorizing each curve, pressing her into the cradle of his thighs. "When, Anya? When will you come away with me?"

Anya threw caution to the wind. "Soon," she whispered, "very soon."

Chapter 5

ANYA HAD NEVER felt more alive. Swooping around the
bends of the road into Helen the next morning was like
flying, her body feeling light and supple, her little car
responding to her sure touch. Her doubts were gone,
swept away by Brady's last passionate embrace, de-
stroyed by the hunger of her own that had blazed into
her promise to him. She had said soon, but on this bright,
cool morning, soon didn't seem nearly soon enough.

Parking in her usual place, Anya walked briskly
through the early morning quiet of the Alpine village
toward the Postons' shop. She was wearing a narrow
black skirt topped by a white silk blouse, her upper body
swallowed by a bulky emerald-green sweater. In her ex-
uberant mood, she had added a fluttering tangerine scarf
for a bright streak of color. She was quite sure Brady
would seek her out sometime during the day, and she
wanted to look her best.

In the cool, still air, the fragrance of roses and spicy
geranium leaves rose from the carefully tended box gar-
dens along the colorful street. Anya liked this hour of
the day, when the streets were swept clean and nearly
deserted, and she sniffed the drifting odors apprecia-
tively, half smiling until she came within sight of the
shop. Then she slowed, wondering. There were never
customers at this time of day, but standing patiently in
front of the shop were two men.

Anya wondered at her sudden feeling of presentiment.
Other shop owners were about, sweeping around their
doors, stopping to chat with one another. There could be

no danger, so why did she feel disturbed? Staring at the men, she realized that it must be because they looked so out of place on the gay little street. Somberly dressed in three-piece dark suits, they were hardly the ordinary, brightly hued and casual type of tourists. Then she smiled to herself and quickened her pace. Of course! They had to be the two men who had visited Roger and Marilee last night and had now come to talk to her, hoping for more information about the Bruner music box. She went on, her green eyes studying them covertly. Then her lips curved into a welcoming smile as she came up beside them and inserted her key in the door.

"A good start for the day," she said cheerfully, "customers waiting."

The men both laughed, a soft, conventional sort of a chuckle, and followed her in, standing and waiting politely as she turned on lights and unlocked the register.

"Now, gentlemen," Anya said brightly, coming back toward them, "what can I do for you?"

The taller man cleared his throat. "Mrs. Poston tells us that you know the man who bought the Jacob Bruner music box and that you might be able to put us in touch with him. We are interested in making an offer for it."

The man's eyes were calm and expressionless, there was absolutely nothing in his tone but a courteous interest, yet Anya felt chilled. "The man who bought it didn't keep it," she said slowly. "It is now owned by a—a collector." She stumbled over her next words. "Unfortunately, in—in the interest of preserving the privacy of our customers, I can't tell you the collector's name." She watched both sets of eyes narrow and thought miserably how deceptive she was becoming. But she certainly didn't want to mention Morgan's name until Brady had had a chance to straighten that out. He felt too responsible for Morgan's trickery. "However," she added quickly, "Mr. Durant—he's the original buyer—does know of your interest. He's meeting with the collector today, and I'm sure he will ask her if she'd like to sell it." She wasn't at all sure of that, but with the cool eyes on her it seemed a good thing to say.

"When will you know?"

"Oh, today," Anya said hastily. "I expect him around noon."

The taller man nodded and looked at his companion, who pulled a card from his pocket and handed it to Anya. "Alpenhof Motel, Miss. Just tell Mr. Durant to come directly to Unit Twelve." He smiled, managing to look quite friendly. "Whether the collector wishes to sell or not, we would like to see Mr. Durant. We can make him an interesting offer."

"I'll tell him," Anya promised, and then, mindful of her job—after all, she was supposed to be selling—she offered to show them the other music boxes. This time they both smiled, rather disparagingly.

"We—that is, our clients—are interested only in the Bruner box," the taller man said. "Sorry, Miss."

Anya watched them stalk away along the flowery street, two solemn crows in their dark suits, and thought how ridiculous it was that a useless object like that old music box could claim the attention of two serious businessmen, and then promptly forgot it, turning to greet a chattering trio of tourists entering the shop.

At a quarter to twelve, Anya glanced past a customer's shoulder and encountered Brady's blue gaze. How a man as big as he was moved so silently she didn't know, but he was there, waiting quietly and holding a package—a package the size and shape of the music box. Which didn't seem important. Nothing seemed important except how she felt, seeing him. She felt immersed in a soft, swirling cloud of warmth shot with lightning flashes of joyous excitement, and that was a dizzying experience. But delightful. She gave him a quick smile and tried to concentrate on what the customer was saying, a mono- logue about bisque dolls that seemed interminable.

"Excuse me." Tired of waiting, Brady had come up and broken in. Anya turned to him in relief.

"Yes?" Oh, how she meant that *yes*. Yes to every-thing—Brady, life, love, taking chances...

"The buyers," Brady said simply, his eyes warm on her glowing face. "Do you know how I can find them?"

"Oh!" Anya glanced at the customer, who was turning away. "I'll be with you in a moment, ma'am." She thrust a slim hand in her pocket and came up with the card, handing it to Brady, glancing at the package in his hand. "Are you really going to sell it to them?" she asked in a whisper. "Won't Morgan be furious?"

Brady's eyes met hers with a look of pained disgust. "She finally admitted ordering it and agreeing to pay the full amount," he said in a low tone, "but she refuses to make up the difference. She says there's nothing wrong with getting a bargain no matter how you do it. So I took it."

Anya drew in her breath. "How?"

Brady shrugged. "Tore up Whit's check, picked it up, and walked out. Morgan did a lot of foul-mouthed screaming, and threatened to call the police. I pointed out to her that I had proof I had bought it and she didn't. That stopped her." He looked past Anya and saw that their whispered dialogue had lasted too long for the wait-ing customer. The outside door was closing behind her. He looked back at Anya with a wry smile. "I'd better get out of here before I ruin your sales. I'll see those men and come back. When can you get away?"

"Soon," Anya said, and blushed at the very word. "That is, Marilee will be taking over before one o'clock." She saw him check his watch and added hastily, "That isn't time enough for you to see the buyers, but I—I'll wait for you." Her face grew warm under his suddenly searching gaze; her lips parted in a quick gasp as he bent and brushed a feathery kiss across them.

"Annie Anya," he whispered, "I'll be back as fast as I can."

It still took two hours. Marilee was behind the counter and Anya was showing a piece of Venetian glass to an elderly woman when Brady came in, minus the package. He went directly to the counter and handed Marilee an envelope.

"The rest of the agreed-on price for the Bruner box," he said, his words barely audible to Anya. "Anya will explain why I felt obligated to get it for you." He shook his head as Marilee started to protest. "No argument. It's yours." He swung around and caught Anya's questioning look. He grinned, his dark face lighting up. "I'll be in the van."

"Ten minutes," Anya said breathlessly. "Maybe fifteen." She turned back to her customer as Brady left the shop. "You need to talk to our expert on Venetian glass," she said firmly, and led her to the counter, handing the piece of glass to Marilee. Marilee smiled mechanically and gave Anya a wild look.

"Durant said you'd explain about this money."

"Tonight," Anya said, still firm, "when I get home." She gave Marilee a small smile. *"If* I get home." She grabbed her purse and was gone in a flick of black skirt and a swirl of green sweater.

Anya came angling across the street toward the van where Brady sat waiting, her slender feet tracking precisely through the crowd, her dark hair lifting and bouncing, eyes glinting emerald as she looked up and saw him watching her. She gave him a gamine grin over the top of the bag she carried, a large bag with the insignia of the Bavarian Food Stall emblazoned on its bulging side.

"There," she said, a trifle breathlessly, and pushed the bag into his arms as he stepped out. "The only thing different is a bottle of wine. All right?"

Staring down at her, Brady shifted the bag to one arm. "Of course. But are you sure you want to brave the outdoors? It's supposed to rain later."

Enveloped in his warm aura, Anya felt a certain tension in his long, muscular body, heard the question behind the question. He didn't want today to be just a repeat of the first time, and, for that matter, neither did she. But how could she tell this man she wanted to be *alone* with him, not just together in some crowded restaurant or motel? Her eyes flickered away from that deep blue laser beam and settled on the middle button of his shirt.

"Does the van leak?"

Relaxing, Brady turned and swept her up through the open door, shutting it, looking through the window at her with a hint of warm laughter in his eyes. "It does not. In fact it can be very cozy in wet weather."

Anya smiled and leaned back in the enveloping seat. That had been easy enough. Brady had understood without questions. She watched him climb in and put the bag in the small kitchenette and wondered if he knew how she had agonized over taking the initiative, buying that bag of food and presenting herself as a willing—no, better make that eager—lover. Probably he didn't. He made his own decisions fast and without regret. Like selling the music box. She bit her lip, thinking of Morgan.

"Did you really sell the music box to those men, Brady? I know you brought the extra money to Marilee—but is it really gone?"

Brady's face hardened into stillness. Swinging out into the busy street, he concentrated on the traffic. "Stop worrying about Morgan, love. The box was never really hers. You sold it to me, remember?" He gave her a quick glance and a tight smile. "Let's both forget it. The damned thing has been nothing but trouble."

"You're right," Anya conceded. With relief, she kicked off her shoes and folded her long legs beneath her, relaxing. He was right, after all. Morgan had been unethical and he had straightened it out. And that was the end of it. She settled back and looked over at him, catching his eyes on her, his rough-carved face softening. She smiled and looked away, swallowing the catch in her throat. She was fully aware of those quivering antennae in the air between them.

Less than an hour later, the van grumbled down the

same steep incline and stopped by the same copse of huge trees. Brady switched off the ignition and reached for Anya, lifting her across the space between them, and then, somehow, into his lap, wedged between his wide chest and the steering wheel. Their mouths met in almost frantic hunger and then softened, moving together in deeply sensuous searching.

Her arms wrapped tightly around Brady's rangy shoulders, Anya could feel his big hand pulling the tails of her silky blouse from her skirt, searching upward beneath it, roving the soft bare skin of her back. When the hand began moving around her rib cage, she knew where she wanted it. The skin on her breasts tingled in anticipation. She arched away, giving him access, leaning back hard against the wheel. The sound of the horn blasting the quiet woodland startled them both.

"There must be a better way," Brady muttered, clutching her to him so the sound would stop. Anya was laughing, and his wide mouth quirked up unwillingly. "How did I get you in here? I must have been desperate." His grin widened sheepishly. "Yep, I remember—I *was* desperate." He kissed her again and levered her up on her feet, unfolding his long legs and standing up to loom over her. "I still am."

Warm and shaken, Anya moved away uncertainly. The space around them was vibrating with tension, a supercharged, primitive atmosphere completely new to her. There was something in Brady's eyes, in the lean body tense as a drawn bow, that filled her with a delicious fear. "The—the food," she stammered, and stepped down into the kitchenette, reaching for the bag.

Brady's arms slipped around her from the back, pulling her rounded buttocks against his aroused loins, cupping her full breasts in broad palms, fingers kneading possessively.

"I'm not hungry for food, love."

The husky sound of his deep voice and the hot, hard length of him against her slender back swept away the last of Anya's purely instinctive female resistance. With a small, whimpering sound, she turned in his arms, her parted lips accepting his plundering mouth, her hands slipping around his sinewy waist.

"Brady..." It was only a breath, sighing out from her dizzying need for him, signaling surrender. His fierce response crushed her against the cabinet, squeezed the air from her lungs, sent her senses reeling from the sheer power of his arms and the intensity of the kisses that moved from her mouth to the cleft of her breasts. Then he gentled, easing the pressure and raising his head to gaze down at her flushed face and panting mouth. He was breathing hard, trying for control.

"Time for us, Annie Anya." He straightened, drawing her away from the cabinet and turning her toward the back of the van. "Come to my bed, love."

The padded benches she had thought would make up into a bed were only benches, but in the rear of the van, behind what she had thought was a curtained area of storage, was a bed already made up, with a pile of cushions and curtained back windows. A small bed, but big enough. It waited invitingly as the cool breeze lifted the curtains and swirled around her while Brady undressed her.

He whispered to her. Love words in her ear and a nip on her neck as he tossed aside her scarf and sweater, a husky growl of pleasure as he unbuttoned her blouse and freed her breasts from the confines of her bra. He bent and suckled, and the rasp of his rough tongue, the sight of his dark, craggy face at her white breast, sent liquid flame to pool deep inside, swelling her loins with exquisite pain. Anya trembled, unsure of herself, helpless in the grip of emotions she didn't recognize. This was entirely new to her, this swirl of pure male passion that Brady emanated, that her body reacted to with aching breasts and weakening thighs, with a wild urgency to be fulfilled. She desperately wanted his bare skin against hers, and her hands went to the open neck of his shirt, fumbling with buttons.

He straightened, waiting, watching her soft, flushed

face, the huge eyes like dark jade, the parted, sensual lips quivering with desire. When she pulled his shirt apart, he drew her to him, reveling in the feeling of her taut breasts against the crisp mat of hair on his chest. When she made another husky sound and clung to him, winding her arms around his neck, his hands dropped to unzip her skirt. Slowly but efficiently, he began peeling skirt, half slip, and pantyhose down in one smooth motion, bending, kissing first her breasts and then the smooth satin of her belly.

Gasping, Anya braced a hand on his shoulder as he reached her feet, stepped out of her high-heeled pumps, held each foot as he removed the hose, and then she stood naked before him, staring in confusion as he straightened again.

"You're so *tall,*" she whispered.

Brady laughed hoarsely and picked her up, holding her high, face to face. "Better?"

She leaned forward and kissed him, openmouthed, her eyes closing in pleasure, feeling him bend to put her on the bed. The pillows were soft and cool against her warm back, and he was whispering again.

"So beautiful you are, love. So soft and tender. Maybe I want you too much." Still wearing his boots and jeans, his shirt open and hanging loosely around his muscular torso, he eased down on the side of the bed and ran his hands over her gently. Slowly, he shaped the full breasts and narrow waist, the almost imperceptible flare of her slender hips. His eyes were their deepest blue, his craggy face tense and serious. Inches away, his gaze locked with hers. "Are you *sure,* Anya? Do you want to give yourself to me?"

She wasn't sure of much, but she was sure of that. She nodded, moistening her lips with the tip of her tongue. "I've already given myself to you," she whispered. "You just haven't taken me yet."

His mouth came down on hers fiercely, his hands burying themselves in her hair, his lips and tongue ravishing her mouth. "You'd better mean that," he muttered.

"I want all of you, all for me..."

Coming out of his clothes, Brady was awesomely male, all hard-muscled length and potent virility. Anya's body reacted with a throbbing excitement at the sight of his aroused loins, and as he slid into the bed, she drew him into the soft cradle of her thighs, wrapping her long legs around his, her slender arms around his broad back.

"Now," she whispered, "please..." She arched, her hips trembling with desire, and felt him fill her slowly and completely, crowding the wildly wanting emptiness with thick, delicious heat. She moaned with pleasure and shut her eyes, concentrating every sense on that joining.

With a last, subtle pressure that knitted them tightly, Brady was still, panting. His arms half supported his heaving chest, and his mouth moved over her warm face with sensual caresses, licking the corners of her parted lips.

"Much too soon." His murmur was drugged with passion. "I wanted to make love to you."

"You are," Anya said indistinctly, "oh, you are, Brady. Lovely love..." His kissing was adding fuel to the building fire inside, the exquisite tension growing around his pulsating heat. "Scary," she added almost inaudibly, "it's ...it's scary to feel like this." She moved, rippling against him involuntarily, and heard him groan.

"Oh, love...don't...what you're doing to me..." His arms slid beneath her, gathering her up, the muscles of his back bunched against her palms. "Ah-h-h, darling..."

Like flying. Like dancing. Like their bodies ignoring their dazed minds and communicating on a deeper level. Demanding and giving, asking and answering, building pleasure on indescribable pleasure in perfect accord. They made sounds, incoherent but warm, they kissed breathlessly as the fountain of pleasures grew higher and higher, cried out together as it burst and spread rushing waves of pure, ecstatic sensation over them both. Then, slowly emerging from the dream, Anya felt the weight of Brady's body ease away. She turned and looked at him, her green eyes glistening with tears.

"I f-feel like a fool," she said brokenly. "I never knew m-making love could be like this."

"It will be better the next time."

She stared at him with a new look of disbelief in her eyes. There was a look of brooding tenderness on his creased face, a warm promise in his blue gaze. Anya sighed, touching the firm lips with a fingertip.

"I don't see how." And that was true. The way Brady had made her feel was far beyond her experience. Her blood still thrummed with it, and she felt an entirely new feeling of having been part of someone else. "It couldn't be," she added firmly, and then indignantly covered his mouth with her palm as he laughed.

"We were like kids," he said, kissing the palm, "like a couple of dumb kids, overanxious and undertrained." He was still chuckling, pulling her closer, nuzzling her hand aside to kiss her throat. "And, God, it was wonderful! Don't ever leave me, Annie Anya."

She wouldn't; she knew that. She would never leave him as long as he wanted her with him. That would be the key—as long as he wanted her. She would have told him, except that her mouth was otherwise occupied, and then the thought of telling him faded in a sort of bemused wonder. Incredibly, she was feeling a stirring of fresh desire, brought on by the magic of a hard, calloused palm on the silky smoothness of her belly.

Later, having discovered and made use of the narrow cubicle of Plexiglas that housed his shower, she dressed adequately in one of Brady's shirts, a deep blue one that covered her from neck to mid-thigh. She sat with him on one of the benches and shared the sandwiches and wine. Rain splattered against the windows, wet leaves swirled past in gusts of wind.

"You were right," she said in vast contentment. "This is a very cozy place in wet weather."

"It's never been quite this cozy before," Brady said, pouring more wine. "I don't want to take you home, not tonight. Do I have to?"

Anya laughed suddenly, her face bright with amusement. "No. Marilee will be delighted if I don't show up. She's been trying to push me into—into some kind of a relationship ever since I arrived." She leaned back, curling into his encircling arm. "I'll stay," she added softly. "I want to stay. But I'll have to be back in time to open the shop in the morning."

Brady's arm tightened and hugged her to him. "That will work out. I'm leaving Helen tomorrow and I'll be back Friday. I'll pick you up Friday at noon and bring you back Sunday night." He sounded perfectly confident, but his eyes, slanting down at her, were not quite so certain. "All right?"

Anya hesitated. She wanted to ask him where he was going and what he was going to do, and that was a horrible thing. How could she even think something so possessive, so prying? It was easy, she thought dismally. She wanted to know every thought he had, every plan he made.

"What are we going to do from Friday until Sunday night?" she asked instead. At least that part concerned her and she had a right to ask.

"What do you think?" Brady's slow grin built from his firm mouth up the creases of his tanned cheeks and into the deep blue of his eyes, then turned into laughter at her abashed expression. He dragged her across his lap and kissed her. "Ah-h, that blush! I love it—how far down does it go?" He began unbuttoning the flannel shirt, and Anya stopped him, holding the edges together.

"Leaving out the lechery," she said, trying to sound outraged, "what are we going to do?"

Smoothing back her hair, he looked down at her with his grin fading. "We're going to find out what you think of the way I spend half of my life," he said soberly. "We're going to the mountains."

* * *

Toward dawn, Anya awoke to silence. The wind and rain had ceased; the chill of a mountain night had descended. But she was warm in the semicircle of Brady's sleeping body and their cocoon of blankets. She lay there thinking of how they were together and how she could never go back. She could never be that Anya Meredith again, closed away and invulnerable, safe from hurt. Always, with Tom, there had been that place inside her heart she had kept for herself alone. A secret place he couldn't enter. That had been her safety, and when he had left, it had been useful. She could smile and walk away.

But it was gone, now. She twisted restlessly and felt Brady's hand soothe her, even in his sleep. It was marvelous and terrifying, the way she had felt herself part of him, the way all her defenses had fallen and let him into the remote recesses of her heart. A man she barely knew. A stranger. This could end tomorrow.

Still, settling closer against his warmth, she thought sleepily that it might be worth it even if it did.

Chapter 6

"ALL I CAN say," Marilee said, "is that you look indecently happy." She poured another cup of coffee and sat down at the kitchen table, where Anya was drinking hers. Marilee's eyes were the same sparkling, alert brown as those of a hungry sparrow, searching for crumbs. Her black curls vibrated, trying to pick up clues. "And I suppose you aren't going to tell me a thing."

Anya grinned at her. "You told me yourself that Brady Durant was an interesting, creative person. What can I say, other than that I agree with you? I had a very nice time last night, and next weekend he's invited me along on a trip to the mountains. He's going to paint, and I—well, I'm going to take some books I've been meaning to read."

Marilee groaned. "You are positively the dullest conversationalist I have ever known." She sat glaring at Anya speculatively, and then brightened. "But you do have to tell me one thing—Brady said you would. What was all this about the extra money for the Bruner box? I feel guilty taking it. After all, he paid what we asked."

Anya frowned. She had forgotten about the money—about Morgan, about Elisha. Because she had wanted to forget. "He would have felt guilty if you hadn't taken it," she said slowly. "He came in to get it because his sister-in-law told him it was there and asked him to get it for her." She raised her eyes to Marilee's expectant face soberly. "She's a collector, and her name is Morgan Whitcomb."

Marilee gasped. "Morgan Whitcomb is a woman?"

Anya nodded. "The name throws you, doesn't it? But she's definitely a woman, and very beautiful. When Brady discovered she had ordered it, neglected to pick it up, and then sent him to get it, he was furious. He thought she should pay what she agreed to pay."

"Well, so do I!" Marilee burst forth indignantly. "I'm glad he made her come up with the rest of it. The very idea!" She got up and began clearing the breakfast dishes away. "The witch! Waiting until we were desperate enough to lower the price..." She went on, muttering imprecations and putting dishes in the dishwasher with angry little slaps. "What a lousy, cheap trick..."

Anya opened her mouth and then closed it again. Marilee had accepted the money as due, but if she knew that Brady had taken the music box away from Morgan and made a sale on his own, she would consider that the profit was Brady's. Marilee had a very strict sense of business ethics. So why tell her?

"Whitcomb?" Marilee said suddenly, turning to peer at Anya. "How can a Whitcomb be a sister-in-law to Durant?"

"Brady was married to Morgan's twin sister," Anya said patiently. "She—died."

"Oh." Marilee's lively face fell a bit. "Well. I didn't know Brady had been married, but then I suppose it's natural. A man that old..."

"He's not 'that old,'" Anya said defensively, and then blushed.

Marilee grinned wickedly, her brown eyes lighting up. "I'll just bet he's not," she breathed. "Tell me about it."

Anya's chair scraped hastily across the floor as she got up from the table. "I'd better be getting down to the shop," she said, consulting her watch. "I'd hate to be late." She went out, disturbing a game of jacks in the driveway, waiting until Betty Sue had marshaled the three younger children and the three beagles to safety on the lawn, then drove away in the clear, rain-washed air, with her thoughts reverting instantly to Brady.

He had been right. It *had* been better the next time. And even better the next. She grew warm just thinking of how he had awakened her at dawn. "That old," indeed! She wished it were Friday, or at least Thursday, instead of Tuesday. The week was a barren desert stretching before her. Where had he gone? Back to Atlanta? He had never said, but she thought Atlanta must have been his home when he was married to Elisha. Might still be his home when he wasn't living in the van. She knew so little about him. But enough, she thought, rounding the curve that led into town, enough to know he was everything she wanted.

On Wednesday, with the shop bulging with customers, Morgan called from Atlanta.

"Anya!" The light voice, full of charming gaiety, brought Morgan's face clear in Anya's memory. "Darling, I can't seem to locate Brady in any of his usual haunts, and I thought of you! He seemed to like you so much, and I wondered—can you tell me where he is?"

"Why, no. I—I haven't seen him recently, Morgan. He was here early in the week, and then he left. I thought..." Anya swallowed and then went on. "Actually, I thought he was there—I mean, in Atlanta." She hoped she wasn't giving him away. Maybe he really was there, and Morgan would know how to find him.

"Well, he's not." Morgan's voice took on a tinge of irritation. "I've checked all the places he could be here, and no one has seen him. Anya... there was a little trouble—just a misunderstanding—about that music box he bought for me. Something about the price, I think. I want to straighten it out. Is the box there, in your shop?" She laughed a little, and then added sweetly. "If it is, we won't even need Brady. I'll come over for it myself."

Anya was suffused with embarrassment, wondering what to say, her eyes on an impatient customer standing at the counter. "No," she managed, "it isn't here, Morgan."

"Oh, hell," Morgan snapped, the sweetness gone. "Then I'll have to find him. If you see him, just tell him I'm ready to do what he wants." She hung up without waiting for an answer.

Anya went back to her customers, wondering if she should have told Morgan that the music box now belonged to another collector and that it was too late for her to come up with the rest of the purchase price. Telling her would save Brady time and trouble, but Morgan would probably have hysterics. Morgan, she was sure, was a woman used to having her own way.

On her afternoons off, Anya shopped for clothes. New jeans, sturdy short boots, long-sleeved shirts, and a beautiful cream-colored turtleneck sweater that Marilee frankly envied.

"Not that I could wear it," she mourned. "I haven't the figure for it." She eyed the collection of outdoor wear somewhat doubtfully. "If I looked like you do in jeans," she added, "I'd wear nothing else. But I've never thought of you as an outdoor type. Are you?"

"Who knows?" Anya asked airily. "I've never tried it. But I love picnics and nature trails."

Marilee grinned. "The mountains are nature in the raw," she said, "and the trails aren't marked with arrows or equipped with picnic tables. The woods are full of snakes and wild animals. You'd better stay close to Brady—or is that the whole idea?"

Anya went on hanging up clothes. "Speaking of things that lurk in woods," she said finally, "I noticed young Rog coming up alone from the ravine this afternoon. Have they caught those fugitives?"

Marilee frowned. "Not that I know of. That brat. I've told him not to wander away by himself, but he forgets. I'll speak to Betty Sue." She looked at Anya ruefully. "I still haven't told her about the fugitives. I'm sure she'd quit. Do you think I should?"

"I don't know," Anya said thoughtfully. "It seems odd to me that we haven't seen anyone searching for these men. And nothing about it on TV or in the newspapers.

Maybe the threat is over and no one bothered to tell us."

"That's true," Marilee said, surprised. "Maybe I'll call tomorrow and find out. When do you leave?"

"Tomorrow at noon." It was magic, the way Friday had turned into tomorrow. Glancing at Marilee's harried face, Anya felt a twinge of guilt. "Are you going to be able to manage on Saturday?"

"Sure." The brown eyes gleamed. "I figure you won't be available on any Saturday from now on, so I'm having Betty Sue take the kids to play school. Besides, I'm beginning not to believe in those hostage-holding terrorist types. As you just said, if the police really thought there was danger, they'd be doing something." Marilee turned to the door, adding teasingly, "Maybe they ought to ask you for advice, Anya. It looks as if you've captured our most elusive mountain man."

"You take a lot for granted," Anya said crossly. "You know how things are these days . . ." Elusive was right, she thought. Brady was an attractive, eligible man who had managed to stay single for ten years. That took skill, and a real desire to stay unattached.

"Yep, I know how things are these days," Marilee said, slipping out into the hall. "Casual. But you aren't casual, cuz. Don't get hurt."

Good advice, Anya thought, but maybe a bit late. She was confused by her suddenly mixed feelings. Now that the weekend was close, all her certainty was gone. What if Brady just didn't show up? After all, he had managed to stay away from her for three days without even a telephone call. Maybe their night together hadn't meant all that much to him. Maybe she was just another willing woman in a ten-year series . . .

"Dammit, Anya, *shut up!*" she said aloud, and slammed the closet door. "It meant something! It meant a lot. He wasn't bored!" She stood there, staring at the door, fighting the old feeling of inferiority. Then, proving a point, she opened the door again and dragged down a suitcase from the high shelf. She'd be ready when he came for her, the suitcase packed and waiting behind the counter at the shop. She'd look like a fool if she had to drag it home again, but a woman had to have faith in someone, and in her case it was going to be Brady Durant.

The most elusive mountain man appeared at Postons' Art and Antiques Shop at precisely five minutes to twelve on Friday. Her back to the door as she lifted down a framed watercolor for a customer, Anya didn't see him come in. But she knew he was there. Something—either a footstep, a faint drift of scent, or those mysterious antennae—alerted her and spread an exquisite relief, a warm throbbing happiness, all through her. She glanced around at him with enormous green eyes that clearly reflected the way she felt, and, below them, a small, polite smile for the customer's benefit. Brady was wearing the usual boots and jeans, and a flannel shirt that looked very much like the one she had worn. Anya thought him beautiful.

"Be with you in a moment," she said breathlessly, and took the watercolor to the counter, wondering. Beautiful or not, Brady looked tense and a bit distraught. His eyes on her were as warm as ever, but the craggy face was drawn and tight. Now, as she put the painting in a sturdy bag and accepted the customer's check, she could hear him moving around aimlessly, impatiently. Clearly, he was in a hurry. She glanced up again as the door opened and groaned inwardly. More happily chattering tourists, two plump women and a plump old man, but—thank God!—tiny Marilee had been hidden behind them.

"Glad to see me?" Marilee's grin quirked around her whisper as she scurried behind the counter, dropped her handbag, and fluffed her already wild hair.

"Ecstatic," Anya told her fervently. She bid her customer good-bye, picked up her suitcase, and marched around the counter. Brady's dark brows shot up, his grin flashed, his big hand reached for the suitcase handle.

"Beautiful," he said in a low tone, "and that covers everything."

Outside, hurrying to keep up with Brady's long stride,

Anya felt a burst of joyous freedom, a sense of unequaled release, like a caged bird suddenly tossed into a blue infinity of sky. She was breathless with his nearness, the long arm slung carelessly around her, the narrow hip and hard leg brushing against her, the warmth and the scent of wool and skin that intoxicated her.

"I missed you," he growled, tugging her closer. "How could I miss you so much? God, what a long three days."

Watching him open the back of the van and put her bag inside, Anya thought of the next two and a half days with a thrill of anticipation. Two and a half days of freedom with Brady. Alone. No Morgan, no tourists, no inquisitive probing from Marilee, no past and no future. Climbing up into the van, she went on, teetering along in her high heels through the kitchenette and past the benches, heading for the tiny curtained section in the back. She glanced around and grinned at Brady's surprised look as he got in.

"Drive," she instructed, sweeping the curtain across. "I'm changing."

They were rolling out of town toward the north when she came back, wearing jeans, a yellow chamois shirt, and the short boots that she promptly kicked off so she could tuck her legs up under her. Brady gave her a look of warm approval as she passed.

"Jeans were invented for you, love. I'd follow that tight little bottom anywhere."

Anya grinned. The old Anya Meredith might have been slightly taken aback by that kind of compliment, but this one wasn't. "Good. Then I won't get lost. Or, if I do, you'll find me."

Brady's hands gripped the wheel, his eyes swiveled to the road in front of him. "We're both going to get lost, I hope. So lost no one can find us. I'm tired of problems, tired of demands. I need a big dose of being alone with you."

Demands. That made Anya think of Morgan and Morgan's instructions. *Tell him I'm ready to do what he*

wants. She glanced at Brady's tense face and thought:
The hell with it. All Morgan wanted was the Bruner box,
and there was no way, now, that Brady could satisfy that
demand. She would tell him later, when he was rested.
She stretched and leaned back into the comfort of the
big bucket seat, relaxing.

"Time for us," she said softly, and saw his quick grin
lighten his face, his hand leave the wheel and come to
clasp hers.

An hour later, they pulled off into a small roadside
park for lunch, a simple matter of combining dark bread,
ham, and Cheddar cheese from the supplies of food stored
in cabinets and the small refrigerator, and then making
a pot of coffee.

"From the look of things," Anya said, repacking the
refrigerator carefully so the door would close, "we could
stay a week."

On his way back to the wheel, Brady stopped and
turned her into his arms. "Could I talk you into it?"

Anya ran her hands up the flat hardness of his chest,
feeling the warmth beneath the wool plaid, the springy
mat of crisp curls she liked so well against her skin.
"Probably," she sighed, "but please don't. Marilee would
kill me. I've promised to stay and help in the shop until
those fugitives are rounded up."

Brady's smile disappeared. "That may be a long time,
love." He released her, turning again toward the front of
the van. "Better get going," he added. "The last part of
this drive is one I like to make in daylight."

By late afternoon Anya understood that remark. The
northeast corner of Georgia was rugged mountain driving
even on the highways, and when Brady turned off and
went east on a roughly graded trail, winding past sheer
drops and around steep peaks, she was tempted to shut
her eyes. Clutching the door, she watched the fading
daylight fearfully.

"Why did I think we were going to an RV park?"

Brady grinned, shifting into low gear "You can't get

lost in an RV park, Annie Anya."

"*I* could," Anya said with conviction. "I have a terrible sense of direction. Try me."

"Too late." He glanced at her, the blue eyes twinkling. "No place to turn around. Anyway, you'll love this place. Trust me."

She tried to do just that—relax and leave everything to Brady. Just before dark, the mammoth van groaned and rumbled down a steep incline on the rapidly dimming trail and ended on a grassy plateau overlooking a shallow gorge and a rushing, rapids-filled river. Brady shut off the engine and sighed with satisfaction.

"We're lost," he announced. "Not another human being within miles. What do you think of it?"

"Stupendous," Anya said, awed. She opened the door and slipped out, shivering in the cool air. In front of them, the rocky, shadowed gorge echoed with a tumbling roar of swift running water; behind them and encircling them were the dark, silent pines, the beeches and maples, their changing colors fading in the twilight. Faint stars appeared in the deepening eastern sky as she watched, and then a drift of even cooler air wavered up from the gorge. She wrapped her arms around herself, hugging the warmth of the chamois shirt to her skin, and felt Brady's arms enclose her from behind.

"You realize, of course," he said in her ear, "that now I have you in my clutches."

Anya had been feeling slightly intimidated by the wildness around her. His warmth and silly humor were more than welcome. She leaned back against him and chuckled. "You aren't much of a villain," she murmured. "You're supposed to address your victim as 'me proud beauty' and twirl your mustache..." She gasped in pretended outrage as he swung her around, put her slim hands on his chest, and strained away from him. "Sir," she said haughtily, "you're forgetting yourself!" In a split-second, she was crushed to his chest as he took her mouth roughly, one hand buried in her thick hair, the other sliding down to grip a slim buttock encased in denim. How did he move so fast?

"Don't tease me, love," he muttered huskily. "I need you too much."

Yielding, Anya allowed her body to flow against his, slid her arms around his neck, and twined her fingers in his rough hair, her mouth open and accepting. "I need you, too," she murmured when he let her breathe. She felt some of the tension go out of him, saw his grin flash momentarily in the growing darkness. He relaxed his grip on her a little.

"Even if I'm a villain?"

Anya laughed. "In my scenario, you're the hero," she said, "rescuing the heroine from lions and tigers, mad bull elephants and pythons that abound in this forgotten land." She leaned back and flung her arms out melodramatically. "Take me, I'm yours."

Brady swept her up, cradling her to his chest. "That," he said, "is the best offer I've ever had. We'll eat later."

Chapter 7

ANYA WOKE UP alone in the small bed, her naked body warm under blankets that had been securely tucked around her. She blinked sleepily at the golden light pouring in through a side window. The sun was long up, she decided. She had overslept. She couldn't imagine how Brady had managed to get up, tuck the covers around her, and leave without waking her. But, remembering the smooth, quiet way he moved, she knew it was possible. She lay there thinking just how coordinated that long, lean body was, and felt even warmer. She listened, but there was no sound of movement in the van. Not a footstep or a rustle. No Brady.

She glanced around and saw a thick, navy blue wool robe draped across a stool where she couldn't help but see it, obviously put there for her use. He had put it there and left. But where had he gone? The scene from the night before flashed across her mind. The looming mountain slopes, the gorge, the rushing, rock-filled river . . . wild and remote.

Surging up and out, leaving the blankets in a tangled pile, Anya frantically grabbed the robe and wrapped the heavy folds around her. Half stumbling, she ran through the van to the wide expanse of glass in the front and looked out, sagging in relief. There, near the edge of the gorge in the distance, was Brady. His black hair glinted above a red-and-black-plaid shirt, his long legs were encased in worn jeans and the inevitable boots. His back was toward the van, and as he moved slightly, Anya could see an easel and canvas in front of him.

Well, of course, he was painting. That was what he *did*. She turned back into the kitchenette, biting her lip. Granted, it was all new to her—this wilderness, the possiblity of danger, and the impossibility of finding her own way back without him. But that was no excuse for being a coward. Which you are, she told herself sternly. The first minute alone, and panic. Snap out of it. Still trembling, either from fright or the cold air, she went on to the narrow shower for a quick wash.

"Anya?"

She was pulling the cream-colored turtleneck over her head, so her answer was muffled. But her smile was brilliant as her face emerged. When Brady bent and kissed her, she could feel the outdoor freshness on his firm skin.

"I was about to cook breakfast," she said, "and see if the smell of bacon would bring you in. You go to work early."

Holding her, nuzzling her warm neck, Brady chuckled. "I intended to get back before you got up. Since I didn't, I suppose I'll have to settle for bacon. And eggs. And particularly coffee." He raised his head and looked at her. "Lord, it was good to wake up here with you." He grinned, rumpling her hair, freeing the few gleaming strands that were still caught in the high neck of her sweater. "No phones, no TV, no people, and no way for you to leave. I've got you, love. You can't run away."

"That," Anya said truthfully, "is the furthest thing from my mind." She broke away from his loose embrace and headed for the small propane stove and the coffeepot. Glancing from the window at the rugged terrain of mountains and gorges, she felt an inward shudder. Run away? Good Lord! She'd be lost in minutes, and who knew what lurked in those wild places? Placing strips of bacon in a skillet, she wondered momentarily what lurked in Brady's mind. Surely, he didn't think she'd want to leave? She glanced at him, lounging comfortably at the small table. That powerfully muscled, lean body, the strong-featured, craggy face, the vibrant masculinity that made such a definite impression of strength and confidence. She felt safe with him, but maybe he had his own fears. The corners of her mouth quirked up in sudden amusement.

"What are you smiling about?"

Anya laughed, filling the coffeepot at the small sink. He might look inattentive, but he didn't miss a thing. "I was just thinking of what you said," she told him. "That I couldn't run away. Don't you know that if you tried to leave me here alone in this place, you'd have to scrape me off?"

He sat up and stared at her. "Are you frightened here, Anya?"

"Not when you're around. But—well, when I can't see you, it's a bit scary." She turned away from his too-penetrating gaze, gave a small shrug, and glanced again through the window. "I don't know what's out there, Brady."

"Nothing nearly as dangerous as a human," Brady told her. "Nothing we can't handle." He leaned back again, relaxing, his blue eyes roving over her slender figure with warm possessiveness. "You're safer here than you would be in a city, Anya, and you may as well get used to it. We'll be spending a lot of time in places like this."

"In that case," she said lightly, "I suppose I *will* get used to it. How do you like your eggs?" It seemed a good idea to change the subject before he found out just how cowardly she was. He seemed to be including her in his future, and she was suddenly aware of just how much she wanted that. "Scrambled?"

Brady looked at her, at the big emerald eyes in a face flushed from the warmth of the stove, at the egg in slim fingers poised over a bowl. His own eyes softened, his mouth relaxed into tenderness.

"You choose," he said huskily. "Then it'll be right."

Anya nodded and concentrated on her cooking. That,

at least, she knew how to do.

Later, braving what she considered to be tall grass full of venomous snakes, Anya picked her way across the clearing to the spot where Brady was engrossed in his painting. The roar from the river covered any sound she made as she approached. She halted behind him, absorbing the scene. Here the foaming river twisted off to the west, past a sheer cliff that rose from the tumbled rocks of the gorge, then disappeared around a bend surmounted by a virgin growth of pines. The pines were huge, shadowed, like dark sentinels against the misty outlines of mountains in the distance. Impressive.

Watching, Anya grew fascinated by the way the scene was coming alive under Brady's sure touch. He had rolled up his sleeves past powerful forearms that held the palette and brush as if they were part of his hands. There was no hesitation or indecision, only the swift, smooth movement that characterized everything he did. The paint flowed from his brush, building the scene he saw before him. Anya began to feel a breathless, almost erotic pleasure in the skill of his long-fingered hands and the beauty they were creating. Then, half turning, Brady dropped to his heels to take a new tube of paint from the open box at his feet, and saw her. Rising, smiling slowly, he squeezed paint from the tube onto his palette without taking his eyes from her.

"So, you ventured forth. Getting braver?"

He knew exactly how she felt. She stuck her chin in the air. "You're here," she pointed out. "I'm not afraid where you are. I would have been out earlier, but I thought it might bother you to have someone looking over your shoulder."

Brady laughed. "You won't bother me, Anya. I'll love it. In case you hadn't noticed, I like having you around. I would have asked you to come with me, but I thought it might be better to wait until you felt like it."

Anya felt somehow challenged. He was forcing her to get over her fears by herself, and she wasn't at all sure she could. She stepped forward, studying the nearly finished painting and then the scene in front of them.

"It's like," she said finally, "but not just like . . ." Her eyes narrowed, puzzled. "It's as if you painted it and then painted something else into it. It's beautiful, Brady, but so—so wild." She stopped, the inevitable flush coloring her cheeks. "Listen to the critic," she added, embarrassed by her own boldness. "I don't know a darned thing about art."

Brady's brows arched. "Maybe not," he said slowly, "but you evidently know me. That's exactly what I did. It's the wildness I like. The wildness that lies beneath the beauty." He smiled, turning those blue laser beams on her eyes. "Like with you, Annie Anya. You're so pretty, so delicate and soft, but underneath you're all woman—wild, brave, and passionate." He laughed, watching her eyes widen in shocked disbelief. "You don't believe that, do you? You see yourself as a timid little ex-housewife, scared of the whole world. Not so, love. When the real Anya gets strong enough to take over, watch out."

Anya spun on her heel. "I'm not like that at all," she snapped, trembling. "If—if that's what you think, you're due for a disappointment." Her throat tight, her heart slamming against her chest, she wished she *could* be all those things, and was childishly angry because she wasn't. She was Anya Meredith, coward. "Anyway," she added, "I don't like being analyzed. I'll go make lunch." She strode away toward the van, forgetting to watch either for snakes in the tall grass or bears in the distance.

"If you make sandwiches," Brady called after her, "we could go out for lunch."

Anya stopped and looked back, an emerald glare. "Out where?"

"Exploring. Looking for more scenes to paint." His grin lighted his dark face. "That is, if you want to."

She didn't answer him. Shaking back her hair, she went on, her anger dying away into hopelessness. She could never be what he wanted. She walked slower, a slender figure in the immensity of mountains and sky, her hair shining mahogany in the sun, her head turning as she took in her surroundings. She became aware of the hollow booming of far-off rapids, the scent of pines in the fresh breeze, the yellow glow of goldenrod that drifted in a bright patch against a boulder near the edge of the gorge. It was pretty, and she approached it cautiously, pulling herself up to sit on the sun-warmed rock. There was no hurry. It wasn't noon yet, and she might as well try to get used to this.

The river held her gaze, swirling over and around the red-brown rocks, flinging silver veils of spray high in the air, tumbling and roaring endlessly. Impossible to wade through that, or find a trout . . . Slowly, she let her eyes wander upward to the forest on the other side of the gorge. Deep and dark, mysterious. She drew in her breath sharply. There was an animal there—no, two animals— almost hidden in the trees and watching her. She could make out the bright brown eyes, fixed on her. She stiffened and began edging down from the boulder. With her first move, the doe and the half-grown fawn whirled with a flash of white tails and disappeared.

Anya sank back, smiling unwillingly. *They* were afraid of *her*. Those deer had the same opinion as Brady— there was nothing around nearly as dangerous as a human.

When Brady came into the van at noon, Anya handed him a package of sandwiches and a Thermos of coffee.

"Let's go," she said briskly. "I wouldn't want you to have to paint the same scene for two days."

Brady was very good about explaining things. He identified poison ivy for her and told her that neither snakes nor bears would bother her if she saw them first. Snakes at this time of year, he told her, liked warm, sunny rocks on the southern slopes and the warm leaves on the lee side of a fallen log. Anya's eyesight became acute. She saw several snakes, three of them timber rat-

tlers. When she complained that the sight of them made
her throat close and her stomach turn over, Brady told
her she would get used to it.

"All they ask," he added, "is that you don't get too
close."

"Tell them," Anya said stiffly, "that the same arrange-
ment will suit me."

Her legs were aching and her breathing was labored
by the time they found a promontory over the river that
gave two entirely different views, one up a valley to the
north that was alive with fall color, another downriver
to a small lake.

"Good," Brady said. "I'll make sketches and color
washes of them both in the morning, and finish them
later at home. In another few weeks, the season will be
over. Too cold to paint in oils outside."

Anya, propped against a rock with her aching legs
stretched out in front of her, looked up at him curiously.
"Where's home? Atlanta?"

"Not for years," Brady said tersely. He reached down
and pulled her to her feet, turning her south again with
an arm around her waist. "I have a house outside of
Dahlonega." His blue gaze slanted down at her warmly.
"You'll like it. With you in it, even *I* will like it. Let's
go back to the van."

Anya was silent, trying to understand the meanings
behind his words and the varying sounds of his voice.
Had he left Atlanta because of his grief over Elisha's
death? He hadn't wanted to talk about Atlanta. Dahlonega she knew, a pleasant old town not far from Helen,
historically noted because it was one of the very few
places in the East where there had been a genuine gold
rush. The gold was long since mined out, but the town
lived on it still, with festivals and tourists who came to
pan a few flakes from the many streams. Marilee and
Roger had taken her there one Sunday to see the Gold
Museum and the other attractions, and she remembered
the pretty houses around it. She frowned, following

Brady's broad back down the narrowing path from the promontory.

"I'm trying to imagine you in a suburb," she said, "and I'm having trouble."

Brady's laugh boomed out, starting a squirrel to chattering overhead. "I'm not that close to town, love. My closest neighbor is almost a mile away."

"You're a recluse?" She sounded faintly critical.

"I have been," he answered lightly, turning to help her down a short but steep incline, "but that's changing."

Silent again, Anya gave up trying to figure out his enigmatic remarks. They were so close, physically. She understood his touch, his desires. When their bodies talked, there was perfect communion. But otherwise he hid his thoughts behind a tangle of meanings. He had secrets. Secrets he didn't want to share. Well, she had a secret, too. She was probably in love with him, and she'd be damned if she'd tell him. Following again, with her eyes blurring, she ran into the solid wall of his back with a soft "Uff-f-f!" of surprise.

"Sh-h!" He was standing still, his eyes fixed on a point in front of them. In a moment, he spoke again, his low tone amused but cautious.

"Mama, I believe. And, if I'm not mistaken, Junior."

If he felt cautious, she would be cautious. Anya brushed her eyes clear and quietly raised herself on her toes to look over his shoulder. Her blood turned to ice, her fingers dug into his flesh. For a moment she was sure she would scream. Bears!

Moving with a soft, padding dignity, a huge black bear was crossing their path some hundred feet ahead, leaving the bluff over the river and traveling toward the slope of the mountain. Scrambling behind her was another bear, smaller but not much smaller, full of an awkward energy.

Disorganized thoughts raced through Anya's mind. A mother bear with her cub? Wasn't that the most dangerous kind? And she and Brady were in full view. Her eyes searched both sides frantically. No place to hide, no tree to climb—didn't bears climb trees, anyway? She froze, watching in horrified fascination as the bear stopped, swinging her head toward them and then slowly rising, sniffing the air, rising and rising until she stood at full height on her hind legs, staring at them.

Beneath her digging fingers, Anya felt Brady's shoulders tense, grow hard. But still he stood motionless, waiting. Nothing moved but the younger bear, bounding toward his mother, stopping, turning toward them. He braced his feet, backed up, and whuffed nervously, ready for fight or flight. In one fluid motion, the big bear dropped, swung a huge paw, and slapped the cub on the rear, urging him toward the mountain.

Brady let out his breath, watching the ground-eating, rolling gait of the bears carrying them into the underbrush and out of sight. Then he turned and put an arm around Anya's waist, starting forward again. "Maternal discipline," he said, still amused. "Wonderful, isn't it?"

"Brady!" Anya sounded strangled. "Weren't you afraid?"

"Only of you," he said gently. "I was afraid you'd scream or run. Black bears aren't usually aggressive, but that might have disturbed her. I'm proud of you, darling. You were absolutely quiet."

"Only," Anya said dismally, "because I was petrified."

But back at the van, she was full of a strange exhilaration, full of laughter.

"Hey, it's nice to be home," she caroled. "Let's celebrate." She pulled out glasses and a bottle of chilled wine while Brady boxed his finished canvas and stored it beneath one of the benches. "Dinner at midnight, as usual?" she asked, pouring wine. "Or at some less indecent hour?"

Brady laughed and sat down, pulling her with him. "I like our indecent hours, Annie Anya. First the wine, then a nice warm shower together, then bed. By midnight, we'll be starving, and I'll cook steaks. Sound good?"

"Sounds grand," she said dreamily. "Very efficient. Brady?"

"Hmm?"

"My legs ache."

"I'll fix that," he said, pouring more wine, "right after our shower."

There wasn't room in the shower, but they managed. "Speaking of efficiency," Brady pointed out, "this is the ultimate. We only have to put soap on one of us."

Streaming wet, pressed against the Plexiglas wall by his sheer size, Anya caressed him with reckless, wild abandon. Her slim hands slid sensuously over all of him, seeking intimacies; her curved figure rippled and wove around his bulk; she nibbled at his flesh and licked his flat nipples with a tongue hot with promise.

"What's the matter with me?" she asked huskily, clinging to him. "Am I drunk?"

"Reaction," Brady growled. He was helpless, thoroughly aroused, half amused. "I think what you're celebrating is being alive, darling. You were scared out there." He was aching with need, trembling with it. "Let's get the hell out of here."

She followed him, taking the towel he handed her, thinking dazedly that part of what he had said about the Anya inside might be true. Not the brave part, but maybe some of the rest...

In bed, he rolled her over unceremoniously. "Now, let's get these legs—back muscles first." His strong fingers massaged stiffness into yielding warmth, making her groan with relief. He flipped her over, his eyes dark blue and gleaming, his grin a white slash in the dim light. "Ah, love, I hope I'm torturing you. This is torturing me." He ran hungry hands over her, and then, sighing, began massaging again. Anya stretched luxuriously, arching her slim body, slowly relaxing.

"That feels wonderful, Brady..." She drew in her breath, trembling as his head bent, following the relaxing body down, his mouth hot and open on her satiny belly, sliding lower, seeking. "Brady, don't!" Her hands clutched at his head, fingers tangling in his damp hair. "No . . . please . . ."

His hands moved to hold her writhing hips; his muttered whisper was warm and seductive. "My darling, let me make love to you." Warm breath tantalized a throbbing point of desire; his rough tongue wreathed it gently. A burst of spiraling, joyous sensation exploded from the tender touch, ran through Anya's blood like drumbeats. It was a miniature storm that half satisfied, half increased her need for him. She let out her breath in a moaning sigh.

"Oh, my love . . . my dearest love."

Brady was still, immobile for an instant, and then, as if he could wait no longer, he parted the quivering thighs and swung himself over her. Pressing into the swollen moist velvet of her inner flesh, he slipped his hands beneath her, lifting her to his thrust. A deep sound rose from his chest, a sound of male triumph, a sound of passionate tenderness.

Swept by fire, by her love for him, Anya clung to his broad back, rose to his hungry loins, found and met the long, slow rhythm he wanted. A rhythm that allowed time for little caresses, for erotic love words whispered in her ear. Time to build the joy of belonging together to the ultimate joy of fulfillment.

As his breathing returned to normal, Brady placed long fingers along Anya's delicate jaw and turned her face to his on the pillow. "Say it again, Annie Anya."

Limp, yet glowing in the aftermath of lovemaking, Anya knew what he meant. But she hadn't exactly meant to say it. Her wide, deep emerald eyes opened and looked at him innocently. "Say what?"

Brady stared at her with an indefinable expression. "Say what you said just before we made love. I want to hear it again."

She looked away, pretending to consider. Then she

sighed. "At that moment, I might have said anything, darling. If you'll tell me what it was, I'll be happy to repeat it."

She waited, but Brady was silent. She firmed her jaw stubbornly. He had never said he loved *her*. So, he could keep his secrets and she could keep hers.

Chapter 8

"YOU'LL BE ALL right?" Leaving her the next morning, Brady was doubtful. Not, Anya was sure, because he thought she was in danger. Only because he didn't want her to be frightened. "I'll be back before noon."

Anya smiled. "I'll be all right. I've got a book to read. Just don't start an argument with Mama if you see her."

Brady grinned and left, carrying a sketch pad and watercolors. This time he would go directly to the promontory for the rough sketches he wanted, and he would travel faster alone. This afternoon they planned a new foray downriver along the bluff, and Anya knew her unused muscles wouldn't take two mountain hikes. She watched him disappear out of sight with only a faint trace of anxiety. She had seen the dangers now; they were no longer quite so mysterious and foreboding. The van was a fort, impregnable, and Brady would be back. Brady could handle any trouble he found.

The book didn't hold her long, not with the perfect day outside and her new, strong wish to relate to Brady's life. It wouldn't hurt, she decided, to walk along the gorge as long as she kept the van in sight. She put on a thick wool shirt in green and blue plaid, tucked her jeans into her boots, and stepped out carefully. This natural clearing didn't seem to attract snakes or other wildlife, but she studied it anyway. Nothing. She set out with confidence, drawn again by the roar of the river.

She was coming back, moving easily and pleased by the way the walk had loosened the tight muscles in her legs, when she heard voices. She turned, looking back at the spot Brady had painted, the twist in the river that disappeared around the pine-topped bend. There, shooting out from behind the bend, was a big, bright red whitewater raft, looking more like a flattened, tough balloon than a boat. There were four bearded men riding it, wearing padded leather helmets and orange life jackets, their oars flashing wildly to keep the bucking raft in the current and away from the rocks. They were heavy men, not young, but still strong-looking, and they were yelling, cursing obscenely, and laughing. One of them looked up and caught sight of her, raised his paddle, and shouted something unintelligible, his mouth like a cavern in his bearded face. Then they all looked up, laughing, and bent to their paddles again as the raft slid sideways. In minutes, they were out of sight, shooting down toward the unseen rapids.

Anya went on, thinking that of all the outdoor sports, that would be the last she would choose. Cold, wet, and hard work. A scenic trip with no chance to look at the scenery. She was stepping into the van when she saw Brady emerge hurriedly from the line of trees to the north. She jumped down again and went to meet him halfway.

"Your uninhabited wilderness was momentarily invaded," she said, slipping an arm through his and wondering at his harried expression. "A raft full of men just went by."

"I saw them," he said grimly, "when they passed the promontory. Did they see you?"

She nodded. "One waved a paddle. But at the speed they were traveling and the effort they were putting out, I doubt if they saw me well enough to recognize me the next time. Why?"

"A rough bunch," Brady said curtly. "I wouldn't want them around."

Stepping up again into the van, Anya looked around at him in surprise. "They couldn't stop if they wanted to, not here. Besides, they were just running the river— having fun, if you call that fun."

Brady started to speak and then shrugged, opening the refrigerator and taking out a beer. "Well, they're gone and we're leaving. We'll have to be on our way before dark to navigate that road leading into here." He handed her the beer and reached for another. "Sandwiches?"

"Pastrami," Anya said, "on the second shelf. I hate to leave."

Brady grinned, relaxing. "Ah-ha. You're beginning to like it."

Anya sat down, sliding along the bench to give him room. "Yes. Are we going for another hike, or are you tired?"

"We're going." He squeezed in beside her and opened the packet of sandwiches. "We'll walk south along the bluff as far as the portage around the rapids. I want to be sure that bunch made it."

"You mean they may need help?"

"I mean I want to be sure they're gone." For a moment, Brady's face was like iron, and then he laughed. "Don't mind me, love. I guess I'm jealous of invaders in a place I thought I had to myself."

Anya nodded. Perhaps that was it. Brady had counted on privacy, and suddenly they weren't alone. But somehow she felt it was more than that. There might be something about those men he didn't like. Something he wasn't telling her.

They walked for an hour along the southward slope of the gorge, with the booming of the unseen rapids growing louder. Finally, coming through a straggle of small trees, they found a sheer drop that went down to a sandy shore. A well-worn trail led up the other side of it, into the forest, and toward the other side of a deep, wide bend in the bluff. Brady stood on the edge, staring down at the sand.

"They made it," he said. "There are fresh tracks and a scrape where they pulled the boat up. The rapids begin around this bend, and the river drops fast. They may be miles from here by now." He looked relieved, his blue eyes clear again, his grin easy as he turned back.

"Let's go home," he said, and ruffled her hair, leaving his hand resting casually on the back of her neck. "Those long legs of yours will be tired again."

Anya blushed. It infuriated her, but she couldn't help it—his words had brought back memories of the night before too clearly. Brady laughed and put his arms around her.

"What a lovely shade of pink, Annie Anya. Are you going to keep doing that? You know I can't resist it." He kissed her, taking his time, leaving them both shaken. "Let's go," he said again, "so we'll have some time together before we have to leave."

Along the rocky, uneven terrain, it was easier to follow than to walk beside him, and pleasant to watch his broad back and the taut, muscular legs. Anya fell behind but chose the same path, trying for the same easy stride. It was no place to jog, but the effort, she thought, was about the same. It felt good, breathing the clean air . . .

"There goes the neighborhood." Brady had stopped, looking toward the slope of the mountain behind them. He gave her a wry look as she came up. "I'm not sure, but I think someone's clearing land. That sounds like a chain saw."

Anya listened, hearing the faint sound, a rising, metallic whine. "I thought this was a national forest."

"It is, but there are a few pieces of private land in it," Brady said, then shrugged. "The hell with it. I know other places to go if this one's ruined."

It *was* ruined, with the evidence waiting in the van. In the two hours they had been gone, the van had been searched, torn apart, turned inside out, ravaged. Even the food lay scattered in the sink and on the floor. Bedding had been dragged from the bed, every suitcase and bag emptied. Brady took one look and leaped outside, staring around at the empty clearing and then circling the van, his eyes on the ground. Coming back in, his face was dark with fury.

"That wasn't a chain saw we heard. That was a trail bike. There are wheel tracks." He swore fluently, describing the man who rode it. Then he slammed back outside again.

White with shock, Anya repacked usable food into the refrigerator, watching through the window as Brady followed the wheel tracks to the fringe of the woods. Then she began on the rest, sorting through the clothes, putting the mattress back on the bed. She saw Brady returning, his long stride quick and angry, his face set in unfamiliar hard lines. Then, lifting the pillows from the floor, she looked down and gasped.

"Brady!"

He came in, looked at the gleaming .45 pistol on the floor, leaned over, and picked it up. Anya jerked away, involuntarily.

"It's mine, Anya. And it isn't loaded."

"Oh." She stared at the gun, confused. "Why didn't he take it? I thought thieves always took guns."

"I don't know," Brady said grimly, hefting the pistol thoughtfully. "Maybe they already had all the guns they wanted to carry. They must have enough money, too. I had fifty dollars in small bills in the car pocket. It's scattered all over the floor, but it's still there—as if they couldn't be bothered to pick up such a small amount."

Her legs trembling, Anya sank down on the edge of the bed. "You said *they*. Was there more than one?"

"There was more than one set of footprints," he said evenly, "but only one bike. As if people on foot had met with the bike rider up in the woods."

She knew what he was thinking. "That's impossible," she burst out. "They were gone, Brady. Down the river."

"Maybe," he said thoughtfully, "and maybe not." He was thinking, his temper cooled. "I should have followed along that portage trail. They could have stashed their boat there and come back here. Easy enough, hiking through the woods above us."

"But they couldn't have known we would leave the van."

"No," Brady conceded, grim again, "they couldn't. But it's probably a damned good thing we did." His eyes swept over her small figure worriedly. "Leave this mess, Anya. We're getting out of here, and I want you in the front with me."

She caught his meaning only too well. It brought a chilly feeling of nausea to her. Four or five men, probably armed, would be more than a match for one unarmed man and a woman. She watched Brady load the .45 with ammunition he took from a paneled cache behind the bed, then followed him to the front. She sank into the big seat with a feeling of unreality. It couldn't be true, what she was thinking.

"You expect them to be waiting in the woods." She made it a statement, not a question, and Brady looked at her with his brows raised.

"I do not. They didn't find what they wanted. Why should they try again? I loaded the gun on the slim chance of seeing the bike rider. I'd like to stop him long enough to get a look at him."

"I see." She didn't see at all, but she was full of frightened questions. "What did they want, Brady?"

The blue eyes went flat, evasive. "Who knows? As far as I can tell, nothing is missing. They didn't want money or my pistol. Maybe they just like tearing things up." He started the engine and turned toward the trail in the trees that would lead them out.

Anya scanned the forest tensely as they neared it, half expecting to see men lurking behind the trees. It was quiet, beautiful, and empty. Gradually, her fast-beating heart returned to a normal pace. When they reached the stretch of narrow road that had made her breathless on Friday, it hardly bothered her at all. But she didn't relax completely until they drove out onto the paved highway. Civilization, she thought, law and order. She turned to Brady curiously.

"What will you do? Go to the state police or a ranger station?"

"Neither," he said shortly. "I don't intend to report the incident."

Anya's eyes widened. "Why not? There could be

fingerprints, other evidence. And they should be on the alert with those men around."

"No." Brady stared at the road, a muscle tightening along his jaw. "Nothing valuable is missing, and I'd just be letting myself in for a lot of paperwork and questions. It's over. Forget it." He glanced at her somberly. "In fact, I'd rather you didn't mention it, either. Not to the Postons or anyone else. It's . . . not important." He looked away, and so did Anya, biting her lip.

She wanted to say that it was important to catch a thief. That justice was important. But she couldn't get rid of the feeling that Brady knew something about those men that she didn't know. Something he wouldn't want to tell the police. She hated thinking it. She wanted to trust him.

"All right," she said finally, "I won't mention it. I won't even think about it." She sat back, curling her legs up, forcing a smile. "Why let it spoil the trip?"

"It couldn't," Brady said, and reached for her hand. His fingers closed around hers with comforting warmth. "Nothing could." His grim face softened for the first time since they had returned to the van. "I hope it hasn't scared you off. I want you to like my kind of life. In fact, I want you to love it."

Anya's hand curled tightly into his. "I like it. I'll see about loving it later."

Brady looked at her still-pale face and saw the sparkle of humor returning to her brilliant eyes, the subtle quirk of her mouth. He grinned, relaxing. "Fair enough. How about next weekend? Somewhere else?"

Anya laughed, withdrawing her hand from his and settling back with a tired sigh. "I'll go for that, providing it's definitely somewhere else. No more Raiders of the Lost Van, please."

It was midnight by the time the van growled up the incline to the darkened Poston home. Wading back through the mess, Anya began retrieving her clothes and stuffing them into her suitcase.

"I'm going to go on to Dahlonega," Brady said, handing her a shoe, "and get the rest of this clutter sorted out." He bent beside the still-tumbled bed, picked up a small circle of gold from beneath it, and handed it to her. "Here's an earring—but I don't see the other one."

Anya stared at the glint in her palm and then stuck it in her pocket. It seemed hardly the time or place to tell him it wasn't hers, that it must belong to some other woman who had shared his bed. She was reasonably sure her voice would come out wrong if she did. She closed the suitcase, picked it up, and walked forward, reminding herself that she was a mature, sensible woman and that it would be silly to be jealous of Brady's past.

Following, Brady took the suitcase from her hand and walked her to the door, waiting on the porch while she found her key. In the moonlight, he looked as tired as she felt, but his kiss had the same magic, his arms around her took away the fatigue, and the feeling of his strong, warm frame was infinitely comforting.

"I hate leaving you, love."

She hoped he meant it. She hated for him to leave. "We'll be together next weekend," she said, trying to ignore the days between. "That's isn't long."

"It's too long. I'll call you tomorrow." He hesitated, holding her close. "Could you come to Dahlonega?"

Anya wanted to say yes, but she thought of Marilee, worrying about the children. "Maybe. I'll see." She pulled away reluctantly. "If I'm going to work tomorrow, I'd better get some sleep."

"I know." He touched her cheek lightly. "It isn't far to Dahlonega, Annie Anya."

Inside, she watched from a window as he turned the van around and headed back down to the highway. It might not be far to Dahlonega, but a future with Brady Durant seemed a million miles away. She wondered just how many women in the last ten years had had the same dream. The slender circle of gold in her pocket mocked her with cold reality. Since Elisha, how many women had he been "crazy about"? He was all the lover and companion a woman could wish for, but something held him back. Something or someone.

A light sprang on at the top of the stairs behind her, and Marilee's sleepy voice yawned in the silence. "Is that you, Anya?" She came trailing down in her robe, not waiting for an answer. "You're late. Maybe you'd better stay home with the kids in the morning and let me open the shop."

"I'll be fine," Anya answered automatically. "Sorry I awakened you. Go back to bed." Gossiping with inquisitive Marilee right now didn't appeal to Anya. She had to smile, though. Tiny Marilee, swathed in that voluminous robe, was trying to look dignified and not at all curious. Inside, Anya knew, Marilee was bursting with questions.

"Did you have a good time?"

"Oh, yes. Very . . . uh . . . relaxing." Anya swallowed a hysterical giggle. "A lot of fresh air, hiking . . . that sort of thing."

Marilee gave Anya an incredulous glance. "Really? Well, I had an interesting call Saturday. From Morgan Whitcomb, in Atlanta." She sounded miffed, and Anya, remembering she hadn't told Brady about Morgan's call earlier in the week, felt guilty. She hid the guilt with a careless question of her own.

"So? What was so interesting?"

"The fact that she doesn't have the Bruner box," Marilee said flatly. "I thought you told me she had paid the rest of the original purchase price to Brady. Where did he get that money he gave me?"

Caught. With all her good intentions down the drain. Anya blushed, stammered, and then parried with another question. "How do you know Morgan doesn't have the box?"

"If she had it," Marilee said dryly, "she wouldn't be trying to buy it. She was sure Brady had brought it back here and you just wouldn't tell her. Actually, she sounded half out of her mind. Where is it, Anya?"

"I guess," Anya said miserably, "that Brady sold it to

those two men who came here that night."

"Then the money is Durant's profit," Marilee said implacably. "Why did you tell me he got it from Morgan?"

"I didn't! You took it for granted."

Marilee looked thoughtful. "Yes, I did. Why didn't you set me straight?"

"Because," Anya said wildly, "Brady wanted you to have the money, and I . . . oh, *hell,* Marilee, stop asking questions! I want to go to bed."

"I suppose you are tired, at that." Having had some of her curiosity satisfied, Marilee grinned impishly. "A weekend with a new lover can be wearing. Oh—that reminds me. Morgan asked for you, and when I told her you were gone for the weekend, she asked me if you were with Brady. How about that for nerve? I told her that whom you were with was your own business."

"Thanks," Anya said faintly, "I'm glad to hear it. Now, can I go to bed?"

"Just one more thing." Marilee sounded apologetic. "Morgan said she was coming to see you on Tuesday. She really wants that box."

"It looks that way," Anya agreed. But if the box were so very important to Morgan, why had she taken the risk of her initial stratagem to get it? Increasingly, Anya had a hunch that there was more to the Bruner music box than met the eye.

Chapter 9

ANYA SIGHED, STRUGGLING against some mysterious, silent force pulling her up from the depths of sleep. Try as she would, she couldn't regain the oblivion her tired body needed. Reluctantly, she opened her eyes and looked straight into the hypnotic stare of a pair of round brown ones, topped by a halo of frothy blond curls. Susan—or was it Sara?—gave a delighted giggle.

"You're awake!" the small girl promptly climbed up on the bed and straddled Anya's waist. "You're our mommy today, Annie Anya."

Anya groaned. "Today's mommy will smack your bottom if you don't get off her. What time is it?"

Sara—or was it Susan?—hooted with laughter. "The clock in Daddy and Mommy's room said, 'Brrrinnng!'"

So, at two and a half, who could tell time? Anya sat up, dislodging the twin, and looked at her watch on the bedside table. Ten o'clock. Marilee had done it—left her with the children and Betty Sue and gone down to open the shop herself. Very thoughtful of Marilee, since Anya needed the sleep, but she'd miss Brady's call. "Dammit!" she said, half aloud.

"Dammit!" Susan/Sara echoed, lying on her back and smiling angelically. "Dammit, dammit, dammit..."

"*Sara!*" Betty Sue thundered from the half-opened door. "That's a bad word." She came in, smiling apologetically at Anya. Betty Sue was nineteen, brown-haired, blue-eyed, and pregnant. "I hope I don't have twins," she added to Anya. "I thought I knew where Sara was, but

I guess I counted Susan twice. I'm sorry she woke you. Oh—a man called and left a number."

"Oh." Anya scrambled up and grabbed a robe. "You could have awakened me."

"He said not to." Betty Sue smiled, dragging Sara off the bed. "He sounded nice, Miss Anya. Real considerate."

Anya was halfway down the stairs, heading for the telephone in the hall.

Brady answered on the second ring. "It's twenty-nine miles to Dahlonega, sleepyhead. You must be rested enough to drive that far this afternoon."

Anya sat down in a small chair, shaking a little. There was no hint of yesterday's trouble in that deep, vital voice. "I can't," she said, hating the words. "Since Marilee let me sleep this morning, I'll have to take the shop this afternoon. But I wish I could."

"So do I. I want to show you my house, among other things. How about tomorrow?"

"Maybe. I mean, yes. No, wait." Tomorrow was Tuesday. She brushed her tangled hair from her face and tried to think. "I should have told you—Morgan wanted you to call her Friday about that music box. She called again Saturday and talked to Marilee, and Marilee wants to give you back the money..." God, she was making a mess of this. She finished in a rush. "Anyway, Morgan is coming here to Helen tomorrow morning. To—to see me, I guess."

There was a short silence on the other end of the line. Then Brady said gruffly, "I'll be there, Anya. She's not going to start bugging you. And you tell Marilee the money is hers no matter who has the box. Be ready to come back here with me."

"All right." Anya barely managed to keep from adding a meek "sir." "I'll like that. I'm looking forward to—to, well, to seeing your house."

"I'd like to see you, right now," Brady said, the gruffness gone. "I'd be willing to bet you're blushing."

Hanging up, Anya smiled at Betty Sue, picked up the twin, and hugged her. "I'm glad you woke me, Sara."

The small face frowned. "I'm Susan."

Tuesday was cold and dark, a foretaste of winter. Anya dressed in layers: gray wool slacks and the cream turtleneck, a multicolored vest and a woolly red car coat. At breakfast, Marilee pronounced her gorgeous.

"I don't feel gorgeous," Anya said ruefully. "I'm hating the idea of telling Morgan the box is sold."

"Then don't," Marilee said practically. "You didn't sell it. Let Brady tell her. After all, it's between them. And that reminds me—I'll give you a check to give him. I'm not keeping that money."

"No. After all, that's between you and Brady." Anya laughed, suddenly feeling much better. "Anyway, I'm on his side."

"Then I'll come in early and give it to him myself," Marilee said stubbornly.

In Helen, the banners drooped, and the usually gay streets looked desolate in a fine, misty rain. But the few tourists who did venture out were in a hurry to find gifts and souvenirs before they left. Anya had a successful morning until the rain increased to heavy showers, but the shop was empty when a Mercedes pulled up in front, parking arrogantly in a No Parking area. Bundled in a deep lavender, hooded raincoat, Morgan climbed out and hurried in.

"Anya! How nice to see you again. Isn't this miserable weather?" Shedding the raincoat, revealing a pale lavender wool suit that accented every curve of her petite figure, Morgan was bright with charming friendliness. "What a lovely shop, darling. I had no idea—this is the first time I've seen it, you know..."

Smiling, murmuring a greeting, taking the damp coat to hang on a rack, Anya let Morgan chatter on until she ran down. Then she offered her a chair and a cup of coffee. Accepting, Morgan drew the chair close to Anya's, sat down, and leaned forward eagerly.

"I've brought the full price for the music box with me," she said. "In cash. Actually, you know, I thought Brady had paid the right price when he bought it. It had been so long since I ordered it that I really couldn't remember what it was supposed to cost." The bright, pale blue eyes with their thick fringe of golden lashes stared blankly at Anya, the perfectly formed lips parted to show small, gleaming teeth. "You know how it is— I hardly ever think in terms of money."

Anya smiled. It wasn't hard, since she was genuinely amused. "It's too bad you've had so much trouble," she said diplomatically. Then, not so diplomatically, she added, "Since you mentioned it, why didn't you pick it up earlier?"

"I wasn't supposed to," Morgan said indignantly, and hesitated, her light eyes flickering. "That is, a—a friend of mine had promised to get it when it came in." She leaned back with an exaggerated sigh and sipped her coffee. "Promises. Who keeps them these days? Everyone's so casual." Her gaze roved over the shop and lit on the shelves of bibelots, sharpening. "Why, you have quite a few music boxes, don't you? Mind if I look them over?" She was on her feet, setting the cup down, moving swiftly toward the shelves.

"Of course I don't mind," Anya said, following. "They're all for sale." She couldn't believe it as she saw Morgan's eagerness, the way she pushed the boxes around, searching. She was so anxious to find that silly box that she even hoped to find it among them.

"Very nice," Morgan said flatly, turning away. She faced Anya, most of the pretense gone from her beautiful face. "Where is mine, Anya? And don't tell me you sold it. There aren't many people who will pay that price." Her soft mouth held a bitter line as she waited for an answer.

"*I* haven't sold it," Anya said carefully. "I haven't even seen it since I saw it in your display." She told herself she wasn't lying. She had seen only a package in Brady's hand.

"Brady took it," Morgan said, her voice low and angry. "Tore up Whit's check and just walked out with it. I know you know where it is."

"No, I don't," Anya said truthfully. "All I really know is that Brady brought the extra money to the Postons."

"Oh, come on." Morgan's friendliness had evaporated completely; her blue eyes were like marbles. "You and Brady are as thick as thieves. Tell me where it is."

"She doesn't have to tell you anything, Morgan."

Both women whirled toward the door. Brady had come in without a sound, and relief swept over Anya as she met his eyes. But Morgan was already talking, grasping Brady's rain jacket with a familiar air.

"Thank heaven you dropped in, darling. I've been trying to find you for a week to apologize. You were right, of course, and I've brought the full payment for my music box, but your friend here won't even listen."

"The box isn't here."

"But you said—" Morgan began.

Brady interrupted her. "I said I was taking it back. I paid for it. It's mine." Brady's voice was clipped and stern. "Don't jump to conclusions, Morgan."

Morgan's mouth opened in surprise. Then, suddenly, her face glowed, a smile appearing. "Oh, Brady! I should have known you'd keep it for me until I came to my senses. You've been teaching me a lesson, haven't you? Here, I'll give you the money." She was half laughing, rummaging in her purse, when Brady spoke again.

"Don't bother. I'm—taking bids."

Anya, speechless with embarrassment and then surprise, stared at the rough-carved face that now looked like stone. Hadn't he sold it? Or was he just torturing Morgan with hope for reasons of his own? She looked at Morgan and averted her gaze. Morgan's face was white, frightened.

"Brady," Morgan whispered, "this is more important

than you think. I *have* to have that box. You don't know . . ." She stopped, staring up at him. "Or do you? Maybe you do, now. Maybe you want to drive *me* over a cliff, like Elisha." There was an ugly taunt, an accusation, in the last words that sent shock waves through Anya with its horrible insinuation. She wanted to turn and run from the anger that boiled between the two of them.

Incredibly, Brady smiled. A tight-lipped smile without humor. "That won't work forever, Morgan. Take your cash and go home. Make your bid with the rest of them if you want the damned box."

The beautiful face was ugly with rage and some other, less definable emotion. Fear? "Damn you, Brady! I won't be the only one to suffer!" Her small hand reached out and grasped a thick pottery bowl, swung back with surprising strength, and threw it straight at Brady's head. Anya cried out incoherently and then stared at the bowl in Brady's hand, at the jeering smile on his face. Morgan whirled, snatched her coat from the rack, and was out into the pelting rain, sobbing with rage. In moments, the heavy car went careening down the street.

Anya turned back from the window and looked at Brady. In that moment, he looked like a stranger, like some man she had never met masquerading in Brady Durant's body. Then his face changed, and the blue eyes turned from ice to warmth.

"A nasty scene, love, but she won't bother you again."

Anya's emerald eyes moved over Brady's face uncertainly and dropped to the bowl. "You caught it. I don't see how."

He stepped forward and put the bowl back in place on a table. "No big deal. Hard to miss with something that size." He moved toward her, and Anya stepped back.

"Wait," she said through stiff lips. "I—need to know what this is about. Why didn't you tell Morgan you'd sold the box? It isn't like you to be cruel. And what did she mean about . . . about . . ." No, she couldn't ask that.

Not about driving Elisha over a cliff. She turned away, her heart pounding with a mixture of anguish and fear. What kind of a man was this whom she loved? She stiffened as she felt his hands touch her shoulders, clasping them gently.

"I didn't sell it, Anya. And that's all I can tell you about that. But the rest of it I'll explain when we have the chance." He had turned her to face him, and his face was Brady's again, blue laser-beam eyes and all, the wide mouth half smiling and tender. "I wasn't being cruel, love. I only did what had to be done. Please believe me."

She wanted to. Oh, how she wanted to. But she understood nothing except that part about bids. It had sounded like *blackmail*, as if he were using Morgan's crazy need to own that box to force more money out of her. She looked away, her eyes hot and wet. "Why should I?"

"Because," he said softly, "you know I wouldn't lie to you." He drew her closer, until their bodies touched lightly, and their faces were inches apart. "Because I love you."

"Well-l-l!" Marilee's bright, amused voice separated them with a jolt. "What an excellent occupation on a rainy day, you two. No customers to bother you." She was laughing as she took off her raincoat. "Only little me, and I can leave if you want . . ."

Torn between a wish either to laugh or scream, Anya somehow managed to do neither. She came and took Marilee's raincoat and muttered something about hanging it in the back room to drip. She disappeared into the little storage room hastily, desperate for a moment alone. After disposing of the coat, she went on to the rest room and splashed water on her burning face.

I wouldn't lie to you. I love you. If one was true, so was the other. Or neither one was. She dried her face and combed through her hair with trembling fingers. He could have said it merely to stop her questions. Maybe he hadn't lied about that damned box, but he hadn't told her everything, either. He had let her think it was sold and gone. She took a deep breath and went quickly out and through to the shop, arriving in time to see Brady tearing a check into neat quarters and disposing of it in the wastebasket. He seemed very good at tearing up checks made out to him, which hardly fit the image of a money-hungry blackmailer. Marilee stood looking on, frowning.

"That was a perfectly good check, Brady Durant, and the money is rightfully yours."

Brady's grin was easy. "I prefer to think of it as yours."

Marilee looked at him calculatingly. "Then let me make it up to you. Bring in some of your paintings for me to sell. We'll both make a profit."

Brady laughed, his brows arching. "Quick, aren't you? I might just do that, later." He looked at Anya. "I'll get the car and pick you up here." He was out and gone before she could answer.

"I'm going over to Dahlonega with him," Anya said instead, hastily answering the question she saw in Marilee's eyes. "He has a house there."

"Sounds as if you're getting serious, cuz." Sparrow-bright eyes ran over her. "You look it, too. All shook up. How did Morgan Whitcomb react, finding out the box had been sold?"

"It wasn't sold," Anya said tonelessly. "Brady still has it. But he refused to sell it to Morgan."

"What? Why?" Marilee was bewildered. "Why would Durant want it?"

"I don't know!" Anya said passionately. "I wish I did. Marilee, what's so different about the Bruner box? Why does Morgan want it so much? Where did it come from, anyway?"

"Why, I'm really not sure. I just contacted a dealer in France whom Morgan mentioned in her letter, and he found it for me. It's hard to trace a small antique. Once they're certified and numbered, you can send them any-where. No going through customs or being appraised, because the value is already known and admitted." Marilee's thin face was a study in thought. "As far as I know, there isn't anything at all unusual about the damned thing. You saw it; we both took it apart. What's different?"

"The sound," Anya said dryly, and laughed. Marilee's casual common sense made her feel better. "Definitely the sound. Chopin's piano needed tuning that day." Still smiling, she saw Brady pull up to the door in a small sports car. "Look at that," she added, forcibly pushing the box and its problems out of her mind. "Today we're traveling in style." She grabbed her woolly coat and ran, turning at the door. "See you tonight—sometime."

Slipping in the door held open by Brady's long arm, Anya settled into the luxury of warmth and softly padded leather. Closing the door, she turned and looked at him. Legs folded beneath the steering wheel, rough hair brushing the leather-covered top, he looked huge in the little car.

"Didn't they have your size?"

His grin was a combination of amusement and relief. He reached for her, cupping her head between his palms, his mouth closing over hers. It was a kiss that first made her breathless, then sent her hands around his neck, fingers threading through the rough, dark hair to hold him closer. A kiss that exorcised the demons of doubt.

"Now," Brady said huskily, "as I was saying before we were interrupted, I love you. Completely. Irrevocably. An incurable case."

"That's *very* nice of you," she said shakily. "It was lonely, being in love by myself."

Brady drew in a deep breath. "It's very nice to know you were. But you weren't by yourself. I knew the day we met you were all I had ever wanted. But—well, I still couldn't believe I deserved that kind of luck."

"How flattering." Anya's voice was muffled by his neck. "What changed your mind?" His scent and the taste of his skin were wreaking havoc with her senses. She pulled away from him to look up, her eyes shining. "Why tell me now?"

Brady laughed abruptly. Starting the car, he swung

out into the rainy, deserted street. "Believe it or not, it was something Morgan said—the first real favor she's ever done for me, and she'd be furious if she knew it." He glanced over at her with his face furrowed. "This isn't easy, love. I buried myself ten years ago, and I've just surfaced." He saw her face go pale and added gently, "I didn't drive Elisha over the cliff. She drove herself. Still, she did it because of me, and Morgan has never let me forget it. But today, when she brought it up again, I realized that all it meant to her now was a weapon to use against me. Knowing that made me free. I've done penance long enough. I'm going to live again."

Anya struggled to understand in spite of her own feelings. Settling back, she tried to speak calmly. "That's cruel, Brady. Losing a wife you loved would be grief enough, without being constantly blamed for it."

His rugged face swung to her in surprise. "Loved? I despised her, Anya. That was my guilt. She threatened to kill herself if I walked out on her, but I wouldn't listen. A week after I left, she took herself and her latest lover over a cliff. I felt as if I had killed them both." He saw the profound look of shock on Anya's face and reached for her hand. "Don't judge me too harshly, love. I had plenty of reason to leave Elisha, and I didn't believe she'd do it."

"I'm not judging you at all," Anya said faintly. She had been so sure he loved Elisha, and now she was sure of only one thing: Brady had been carrying a load of guilt and Morgan had been using it as a weapon. "Maybe," she said slowly, "it was only an accident. After all, why would she kill her lover?"

"She didn't die right away," Brady said grimly, and he released Anya's hand, turning onto the highway to Dahlonega. "She lived long enough to get to the hospital and tell Morgan she had done it because I left her. As for the man, I guess he was just in the wrong place at the wrong time."

Wrong, yes. There was something wrong with all of it. Anya's mind was full of disconnected thoughts, mixed feelings. "And ever since," she said, "you've been trying to make it up to Morgan."

"Of course," he said simply, "I had to do something." He shrugged, as if shrugging away memory. "They were so close, as twins are. Morgan was hit hard. She asked me to help her get out of the wild gang the two of them had been running with, and I took it on—hoping to save *her*, at least. I found her a job, new friends—I even introduced her to Whit." He sighed. "Whit won't like me for that when he finds out. I'm sure she's back in— maybe she never really quit."

"Brady," Anya said helplessly, "you're confusing me. Back in what?"

"Back in what they call The Game," Brady said grimly. "Running drugs, hiding bombs, anarchy, war games . . ." He looked at her utterly shocked face and sighed, staring ahead again through the pelting rain. "I'd better start over. I met Elisha when I came home from the service, and her beauty bowled me over. We were married in a month. A week later, she took me along on a camping trip with her friends. I knew them slightly—members of well-to-do families, parasites mostly. But I went along to please her. I couldn't believe what I saw." Silent, he seemed to be thinking back.

"You won't understand, Anya. These men live for the ultimate excitement, the ultimate risk. That camping trip included drugs, casual sex, and war games with live ammunition. A survivalist trip, they called it. One of their milder sports, I found out later. I had to force Elisha to leave, and the next time she went alone. She couldn't give it up, but she still wanted our conventional marriage to hide behind. That was their biggest thrill—moving in the best circles in the city, keeping their other lives hidden, and playing The Game."

Anya's skin crawled. "And you think Morgan is in it? Even now?"

"Either she's doing it, or they're doing her," Brady said bitterly. "One of their specialties is blackmail, and they know Whit isn't aware of her past."

"Good Lord! What kind of men are they?"

"Scum." Brady was dark, brooding. "You saw four of them, Anya. On the raft in the river."

She gasped and was silent while things fell into place. "They knew you were there," she said, thinking out loud. "They knew it was your van." She looked over at him searchingly. "What did they want, Brady? What were they looking for?"

He didn't look at her. "You're jumping to conclusions now. How could they know we were there? They would have searched any van they found, just for the hell of it." He reached over and took her hand again. "It could have been only a coincidence—a bad one. And this isn't the way I wanted to spend the afternoon. I've explained all I can. Now, let's forget it."

"Let's," she said at once. She was more than willing to put the whole, confusing, saddening story out of her mind. She wanted to remember only what Brady had said about love. Those words were engraved in gold. Riding along in silence again, she studied the craggy profile, the long, folded length of him. When she couldn't stand just looking any longer, she reached out and ran a caressing hand along his thigh.

"Incurable, hmm?"

He caught the hand, bringing it to his mouth, kissing the palm. "Chronic, too." The blue eyes slanted over, clear again and beginning to twinkle. "Touch me again, and I'll pull over here and demonstrate the technique of making love in a bucket seat."

"That's impossible."

"Maybe," he said, looking thoughtful, "maybe not. How can you be sure?" He slowed the car, kissing her hand again. "Want to be a pioneer in the research?"

She pulled her hand away, curled her legs up, and grinned. "I can wait—but only if it isn't too long a drive."

He grinned. "With the incentive you've just given me, it won't be."

Chapter 10

THE CAR TURNED off at the outskirts of Dahlonega, taking a northwest route, a rolling road without much traffic on this rainy day. Brady was humming again, that throaty, tuneless sound of contentment Anya had first heard on the way to Atlanta.

"Not far now—another ten miles." He glanced at her with warm possessiveness, a glance that touched all his favorite places, from the black-fringed emerald eyes that dominated her face to the swell of her breasts in the creamy sweater, the slender hips and long legs in gray wool. The car swerved slightly. With a rueful grin, he returned his gaze to the road. "That is, if we get there," he added. "You're very distracting. At least at my house no one will walk in on us."

She knew what he meant. The slight unsteadiness in his deep voice only increased the delicious tension she felt. It took sheer willpower not to reach across and touch him. Their desire for each other vibrated in the air between them, warm and urgent. Anya breathed deeply and tried to relax. Looking through the now-streaming window, she saw only an occasional farmhouse. In the wet gray distance, hills rolled up to mountains beyond. It looked endlessly lonely.

"Are you always alone at home, Brady? Don't friends drop in?" Somehow she was sure he had friends. Friends who meant a lot to him.

"Not unless they're invited," Brady said, and grinned. "They respect my artistic temperament."

Anya laughed. "You don't have an artistic temperament."

"You know that," he pointed out, "but they don't.
Occasionally, I rant and rave a little to keep them con-
vinced." He leaned back and chuckled. "Seriously, only
very good friends know where it is, and they don't in-
trude. I—needed to be alone for a few years."

After Elisha, Anya thought, this had been his retreat.
He was a sensitive man, her lover. But he was reaching
out now, and she meant to be there when he needed her.
She unwound her long legs, stretched hugely, settled back
again, and gave him a brilliant smile.

"I'm glad you invited me."

"I'd like to keep you there," he said, slowing and
turning into a hidden lane. "Lock you in and throw away
the key." The lane wound between trees and rhododen-
dron, obviously a private road.

"A quick ten miles," Anya commented.

"Not when you count two miles of driveway," Brady
said, and laughed. "I suppose it was overdoing it, building so far from the highway, but I liked the site."

A man of definite opinions and one who had the courage of his convictions. One could learn a lot about a
person from his home. She smiled, watching the lane
wind around knolls topped with big trees, through glades
where water trickled down from higher ground. There
was no wind now, only the light, constant rain. Except
for the lane, there was no sign of habitation until at last,
passing through a grove of fiery maples, they came to a
clearing at the base of a hill.

Brady's house, built of mellowed cedar now darkened
by the rain, was wide and many-windowed, with a broad
roof sloping upward gradually and then rising abruptly
into a second story in the rear, giving the impression of
climbing the mountain behind it. It fit the setting, the
effect heightened by the foundation of natural stone and
the native plantings and trees around it. It welcomed
them, offering shelter from the rain with a low porte

cochere at the entrance.

"It looks," Anya said, "as if it grew there all by itself. Natural and—and strong." Was that, too, like Brady? Or did he just have an artist's eye for what would suit the setting? She glanced at him and found him looking at her, not the house.

"Now for the inside," he said, smiling, "which I hope you'll find interesting." He had slowed to allow her a view of the house; now he took the small sports car around and into the porte cochere. Getting out, he came around and opened her door, looming tall beneath the low roof. "I've been looking forward to this," he said, leading her up the steps to a recessed door. "I worked out a plan for the tour on the way here."

Opening the door, he exposed a great expanse of polished floor and a curved staircase rising at the rear, all dim in the gray light that came through the windows. "The tour," he added, wrapping an arm around her waist and starting her toward the stairs, "begins, naturally, in my bedroom. I hope you don't mind."

Shrugging out of the woolly red coat, Anya gave him a sideways glance from wickedly sparkling green eyes. "I don't mind at all," she said sweetly, dropping it on the polished floor and beginning to work on the buttons of the vivid vest as he pulled her up the stairs.

Anya stretched, yawned, and settled down again in Brady's arms. "Love your bedroom," she observed, and let her gaze wander idly over the pearl-gray walls, white woodwork and curtains, the dark wood of chests and tables. The room was subdued and serene, except for the bursts of color in the many paintings. They lit the room with warmth and beauty, like so many small fires. "The bed is nice, too," she added. It was considerably wider than the one in the van, though they didn't seem to be using the extra space. "When do I get to see the rest of the house?"

Brady chuckled. "You must have seen the stairs.

They're supposed to be one of the architectural triumphs of this place. Curved, carved, cunningly fashioned..."

"Only a blur," Anya said, "as you dragged me up here. Who can see at that speed?" She curled tighter into the angle of his lean frame and looked at a window. The rain had stopped, and from the slant of a watery sun it was late afternoon. "You must love living here, Brady."

"I like it," he said slowly. "I like coming back to it, but I've done a lot of traveling...running away." He spoke reflectively, his eyes closed, the thick black lashes lying on his cheeks like velvet on stone. They opened suddenly and stared at her, intensely blue. "I'm through running, Annie Anya. Are you going to help me settle down?"

"I might," Anya said carefully. "We'll see." She was aware of her heart beating. Spending the rest of her life with Brady Durant had begun to seem both dangerous and desirable. Very desirable. Maybe very dangerous. It was just a feeling, but a strong one.

"Hmm. Looks like I have to sell you on the idea." Brady sat up and threw back the covers. "I'll start my pitch by showing you the rest of the house, and then cooking your dinner. Come on, love—the shower here is definitely big enough for two."

The bath was outsized, decorated with gleaming black tile and white fixtures, with thick yellow towels. The shower was serpentine, a tile corridor winding into an oval of polished chrome that reflected misty, shimmering images of their naked bodies.

"It's indecent," Anya complained, "all of us in here together."

"I'll fix it," Brady said. "I'll cover you up." He reached for the soap. Anya watched as the shimmering man slowly and seductively spread lather over the shimmering woman, and knew she had never been happier in her life.

Later, Brady led her across the hall upstairs and opened a door. A north wall of long windows faced them; two easels were in the center of the room, and shelves were stacked with canvases and boxes of paints. "Workroom," he said, "for winters."

Anya smiled, thinking how like him it was to call it a workroom instead of the grander title of "my studio." Not a pretentious man.

Downstairs there were no halls, no closed doors, all open space with a profusion of light from windows and from skylights allowed to stream in through that broad front roof. Beneath the skylights were islands of growing things—palms, ferns, vines, even flowers. Brady had brought his outdoors indoors.

"When you're not here, who takes care of this jungle?" Anya asked, fascinated.

"A couple named Richardson moves in when I move out," Brady said, pulling a dead leaf from one good-sized tree. "It's a labor of love for them—most of these came from their greenhouse. How do you like it—I mean, the whole place?"

"Give me time," she said, though she already knew. Standing there in his red flannel shirt, the jeans riding snug and low on his lean hips, his usual boots planted firmly on the wide-planked floor, Brady looked completely at home in the informal house. But there was more to the place than just his rough masculinity. There was also what was inside that rugged exterior: a feeling for color and balance in the neutral background; the shafts of light; the vivid paintings on the walls. There was sensitivity in the graceful flare of a ceramic vase filled with autumn leaves, and a thoughtful curiosity in the long shelves of well-used books on the west wall. Anya turned slowly, taking in the wide fireplace and mantel, the tops of chests and tables. A few wood carvings, and some good pieces of pottery. "I love it," she said finally. "It's just like you. And I'm not surprised that you don't have the Bruner box on show. It wouldn't fit in, would it?"

His eyes flickered and moved away from hers. "Not in my house," he said shortly. "Now, if you'll step around this screen, you'll be in the dining room."

So, Anya thought, he doesn't want to see or talk about that unmusical music box. She moved after him, passing a gray tweed sofa and chair accented with fat, brilliant red pillows, going around a sectioned, silvery screen and into an area that contained a heavy ebony table and chairs. A matching buffet held a silver vase of yellow goldenrod, silver candlesticks with yellow tapers. Someone—Brady?—had made the room welcoming. But the mention of the music box had struck a sour note. Why?

"The kitchen," Brady said, walking through an arch. "And, the Richardsons have left us a salad from their greenhouse." He picked up a wire basket of fresh-washed lettuce, tomatoes, and a bunch of slender scallions. "Picked this morning, I would bet." He seemed to be making an effort to be pleasant, but his eyes were still distant. Ignoring the bright yellow and white kitchen and gleaming appliances, Anya impulsively challenged him.

"Brady, you're shutting me out. I mention the Bruner box, and all at once I find the door closed on me." She stood squarely in front of him, her feet planted apart, her hands on her hips. "Why are you making such a mystery of it? Why not let Morgan have it—or at least tell her what price you want? You aren't a vindictive man..."

He set the basket down carefully on the yellow counter, his jaw like iron. "Maybe I am," he said slowly. "Maybe that's what I want—revenge. In any case, I thought I had made it clear to you that I wouldn't discuss that damned toy." He caught her arm as she turned away angrily. "Drop it, dammit! It has nothing to do with us."

Anya stood with her face averted, miserably conscious that she had been prying. And not only because she felt shut out, but also because she simply wanted to know. She was becoming as insatiably curious as Marilee, wanting to know everything. But there was something else; some feeling of wariness and danger, which nagged at her. She turned her head and looked up with tears gleaming in her green eyes. "It has something to do with *you,*" she said tremulously. "Morgan threatened you."

Brady's face changed, lightening. "Is that what's worrying you, love?" He turned her into his arms, holding her loosely with one hard-muscled arm around her waist, tipping her face up with a long finger. He kissed her, light and tender. "Tell you what—if Morgan attacks, you can stop her when she hits me too hard. Fair enough?"

Anya had to laugh. Put like that, it did sound ridiculous. "Fair enough. I'll protect you. But if I'm going to fight, I'll need food."

"Nothing simpler," he said, releasing her. "Make the salad while I start the charcoal."

The deck outside afforded a practically vertical view of the peak rising behind the house, the dense forest that climbed in and flowed around them. A brook ran angling past the house, burbling over small rocks. Looking, Anya realized that except for the thin wisp of smoke rising from the grill and the nearly hidden entrance to the lane from the highway, no one driving past would think this section of the woods any different from the rest of it. Even the second story wouldn't show its roof above the tall trees on the knolls.

"I can see why you don't have drop-in visitors," she commented. "Who could find this place?"

Brady grinned. Standing at the grill in his easy stance, he turned the sizzling steaks over and poked an exploratory fork into the foil-wrapped potatoes in the coals. "Only a chosen few," he said. Then he added, teasing, "Morgan isn't one of them. I'm safe."

Anya snorted. "Nice to know I won't have to use my overpowering strength tonight." She was comfortably ensconced in a deep-cushioned lounge chair, a frosty margarita in one hand as she watched him cook. A big salad waited on the cloth-covered redwood table beside them, along with assorted plates and silverware. A truly domestic scene, and she loved it. She wondered lazily if it would ever occur to Brady to ask her if she knew how to cook.

Inside, past the opened sliding doors that led into the house, the telephone rang. Putting down his long-handled fork, Brady went to the doors and shut them. Muffled, the telephone rang again as he came back to the grill. Anya stared in surprise.

"Aren't you going to answer?"

"It's been my experience," Brady said, "that if I don't answer, then after a while it stops ringing." He laughed at her expression. "Right now, I'm with you." He reached for the plates and expertly flipped a steak on each, speared the potatoes, and dropped them on. "Come and get it, Annie Anya."

Anya laughed and swung her feet to the side of the lounge, rising and stretching. Brady's back was toward her as he dished salad into bowls, and the line of his bending body was suddenly irresistible. She slid her arms around his waist and tightened them, moving sensuously against his tight buttocks.

"I'm not hungry for food, love." She managed a passable imitation of his husky voice that day they had first made love.

Brady laughed, a clear, delighted sound, turned, and picked her up, holding her in the air. "Patience, Annie Anya. This time we eat first." Putting her down, he rumpled her hair. "It's going to be fun, living with a nut."

Maybe. Anya sat down, still conscious of the undercurrent of her thoughts. There was no doubt that she loved him, but she hardly knew him. Too many secrets. Eating, talking, laughing, she watched the rough-carved face and wondered. This time, she wanted to be sure before she committed herself.

After dinner, with the dishwasher whirring in the kitchen, Brady built a fire in the fireplace. They lounged on the gray tweed couch and talked on the safest of all topics: their childhood, growing up, things they had done. The fire flickered and glowed, deepening the clefts in Brady's cheeks, shadowing Anya's green eyes as she lay against his shoulder.

"You were a marine?" Genuine surprise colored her voice as she interrupted his tale. "That doesn't sound appropriate for an artist."

"I learned a lot," Brady said meditatively. "Chiefly, that I wasn't cut out to be a peacekeeper. Our unit was specially trained for that, and I spent a lot of time in foreign countries where we were feared and hated as much by the people we were supposed to be protecting as we were by the people we were protecting them from." He smiled wryly. "In fact, at times it was hard to tell one from the other. We learned to be wary and quick to react."

Anya laughed softly. "I've noticed your reactions. But it's still hard to believe you were a marine."

"Oh, yeah?" Brady growled the words out of the side of his mouth like an old movie character. "Well, lemme tell ya, babe, I'm tough an' I'm rough, an' I like my wimmin willin'." Halfway through this ridiculous speech, he had lifted her and tossed her, laughing, on the couch. Sprawling on top of her, he kissed her noisily and then not so noisily, his mouth softening, beginning a gentle persuasion. "In some ways," he added smugly, "my reactions are still fast."

"Any faster," Anya muttered, trying to breathe beneath his weight, "and we'd never make it out of bed." She wriggled into a more comfortable position and took a deep breath. "It's late, Brady."

He raised his head and smiled down at her, building more fire shadows in his creased face, making reflections like tiny flames dancing in his eyes. "This won't take long." His hand slid neatly beneath her sweater and found what it wanted.

Anya sighed, tilting her head to allow his suddenly hot and seeking mouth to find the tender flesh beneath her ear. She could feel a glow, a rising heat from the center of her being. After all, she thought dreamily, it doesn't matter if I get home at one o'clock or two . . .

A loud knocking on the entrance door shattered the firelit silence, and Brady was on his feet, cursing loudly.

"No one knows we're here! So, who in hell is that?"
He strode away rapidly as Anya sat up and smoothed her
clothing. She stared toward the door as Brady flipped on
the outside light, and then flung open the door. A man,
hatless but wearing a long coat, open over a dark suit,
was standing there, clearly delineated by the light.

"What in God's name..." Saying it, Brady stepped
out and shut the door, but Anya was certain that the rest
of the sentence was hardly welcoming. She was also
certain that she knew who the visitor was and why he
was here. Even in that split-second, she had recognized
the calm, expressionless face of the tall man who had
wanted to buy the Bruner box.

She stood up and moved uneasily around the room,
her doubts returning. She felt sure he had come with an
offer for the box, and she wondered wryly how much it
would be, and if Morgan could top it. *"Maybe that's
what I want—revenge,"* Brady had said. She shrugged
and went to collect her woolly coat and handbag.

When Brady came in, Anya was pulling on her gloves,
her face averted. "I'd like to go home now," she said
quietly. "It's late."

Brady nodded and went to get his jacket, his face
grimly set.

As they walked in silence to the car, Anya railed
mentally against the Bruner box. More and more, it
seemed like Pandora's box—a source of discord...and
perhaps worse.

Chapter 11

"YOU NEEDN'T THINK I'm going to ask you any questions," Marilee said, sipping coffee. "I've decided that the things I can imagine going on between you and Brady Durant are a lot more exciting than your answers would be." Marilee had just come back to the kitchen after seeing Roger, young Rog, and Becky off to office and school, respectively. With Steven, Susan, and Sara in Betty Sue's care upstairs, she was ready for a good gossip session. Having delivered that ultimatum, she leaned back and asked, "How did you like his house?"

Anya smiled faintly. "To answer your question," she said dryly, "it's lovely."

"Would you like to live there?"

Looking up, Anya met the round brown eyes and knew the question went a lot deeper than whether she found the house livable or not. "I'm not sure," she said slowly, answering all of it. "I—might find it lonely." She stood up, taking her plate and cup to rinse and put in the dishwasher, her delicate dark brows drawn together, her full lower lip caught between her teeth.

"Brady is different," Marilee conceded gently, "but from what I've seen, I think he cares for you."

"Maybe," Anya said slowly, shutting the dishwasher and turning away, "and maybe not. Or maybe not enough . . ." She looked at Marilee with tears glittering in her big eyes. "At times I'm foolish enough to think I know the man, and then I find out I don't."

Marilee sighed. "If you think you're ever going to

know Brady as well as you knew Tom Meredith, you can forget it. He's a lot more complicated a person. Tom had no depth." She stared at Anya, the brown eyes keen, serious for once. "You have to take some things on faith, Annie Anya."

Anya nodded reluctantly, murmured something about how late it was, and made her escape. It was easy for Marilee to talk—she and Roger were so close they even thought alike. No secrets, no moods...

Driving into town, she went over the trip home from Brady's house the night before. He had been silent and preoccupied, his craggy face grim in the greenish glow from the dashboard of the little car. He hadn't mentioned a word about the man who had come to the house, nor had Anya asked. She wasn't about to make the mistake of mentioning anything that could possibly bring up the subject of the Bruner box. But Brady's mood had made her miserably uncertain by the time they had reached the Postons' home, and maybe it showed, because Brady had taken her in his arms and held her as if he never wanted to let her go.

"I was wrong," he had said. "It isn't quite time for us yet, love. There's something I have to do first—some loose ends to tie up."

That had made her even more uncertain, and she had tried to pull away. He had simply held her still and kissed her into complete surrender.

Her hands tightened on the wheel as she thought of that. And of what had come after it. First he had said he wouldn't see her until the weekend, and then he had asked her to drive over to Dahlonega on Friday and meet him in front of the Gold Museum.

"We're going northwest this time," he had added, "and it'll save time. Do you mind, darling?"

And she had said she wouldn't mind at all! How could she be so weak? No explanation, no excuse—not even a good lie to smooth over his mood or his reasons for shutting her out. She should have told him to stay away until all his loose ends were tied up. She should have refused to meet him on Friday. In fact, she should have run like hell after that first picnic.

Parking the car, she stepped out and smoothed down the neat teal-blue suit she was wearing, remembering his last words to her. "Be careful, darling." It had been a long time since she had heard that phrase, but maybe she should take it to heart. It wasn't too late to run away, and surely Marilee could find other help. But, on the other hand, maybe this weekend Brady would open up and share his thoughts with her. Walking away toward the shop, Anya knew she was clinging to a very slim hope.

Oktoberfest, which the town of Helen celebrated from the first of September to the end of October, was now in full swing as October arrived. Helen's eighteen-bell glockenspiel music came pealing out at eleven in the morning, and again at two and five in the afternoon every day, concentrating now on polkas, beer-drinking songs, and other lively Germanic tunes that continued to ring in Anya's ears long after the bell-like sounds grew silent. The crowds were thicker than ever before, and louder and gayer, especially around the beer-drinking contests. The weather was perfect, and every motel, bed-and-breakfast, and hotel for miles around was jammed with vacationers.

"Best week yet," Marilee said Friday morning as Anya prepared to leave for the shop. "And two more days to go, with the most beautiful weather I remember for October. It's positively balmy." She smiled brightly at Anya, hoping to lighten her somber expression. "You can leave early for your weekend, cuz. I'm coming in at eleven for a meeting with a salesman. I have to reorder."

Anya frowned. "There's no hurry. Brady won't expect me before twelve-thirty." Truthfully, though she was packed and ready, she wasn't sure she wanted to go. More and more, she felt as if she were only putting off a moment of decision. She ached with the need to see

Brady, to feel his arms around her and let his lovemaking sweep her far away from cold reality, into that world of their own. But she knew she couldn't live in a day-to-day world with a man she suspected of underhanded dealing. And there had to be something wrong with what he was doing—or why was he so secretive about it?

Driving into town, wearing only a light blouse with her suit skirt because of the warmth, Anya made up her mind to have it out with Brady this weekend.

At exactly eleven o'clock, the glockenspiel music began its melodious ringing and Marilee dashed into the shop, a thin bundle of energy in her usual bright calico. The shop held only a few customers, most of them "just looking." Anya gave Marilee a relieved glance and picked up her handbag.

"I guess I will leave early. Most of the morning rush is over."

"Ah-ha. The weekend has begun to look more inviting?" Marilee's smile was teasing and Anya returned it ruefully.

"In my present mood," she confessed, "I just want to escape the . . . er . . . music. All that cheerful gaiety." She saw Marilee's brown eyes mirroring concern and felt guilty. "Don't worry about me," she added gently. "I'm a big girl now. At least, I hope I am." She went out, turning to wave and smile brightly. As she walked briskly toward her car, it occurred to her that she had been as secretive with Marilee as Brady had been with her. But there was no way she could tell Marilee about it. Marilee had gladly forgotten the Bruner music box, believing it sold and nestling in the collection of the man who had hired those agents to find it.

In Dahlonega, the streets were as crowded as in Helen, and the parking was scarce. Anya ended up leaving her car blocks away from the center of town, but with time to waste it didn't matter. She wandered in and out of shops, bought a tiny gold nugget on a chain, and, as the hands on her watch neared twelve, she began strolling

toward the large, imposing building that housed the Gold
Museum.

The museum was still a block away when she caught
sight of a shop advertising unusual antiques. A display
of antique clothing brought her to a stop in front of the
wide window. She was trying to imagine a full-breasted,
full-hipped woman with a sixteen-inch waist who would
fit into the Edwardian silk and lace gown, when she
realized a man behind her was watching her. Reflected
in the window, he was standing on the curb and looking
her up and down. She wheeled, catching a glimpse of
pale gray eyes, surprisingly small in a heavy face, and
then he averted his gaze, stepped down from the curb,
and, ignoring the traffic, strode across the street. He was
wearing a green hunter's cap with the usual plaid shirt
and jeans stretched over a bulging figure, and she watched
the cap disappear in the crowd on the other side.

Perhaps, she thought, he had thought he knew her
and then realized he was mistaken. But he had looked
vaguely familiar to her, too. She shrugged. He could
easily have been one of the hundreds of vacationers who
had been in the Postons' shop this last week, and that
would account for all of it. She wandered on and then
forgot the whole episode as a huge green van slid into a
loading-only zone in front of her.

Watching Brady emerge, the long legs first, the lean
body dropping down easily, the blue, blue eyes coming
straight to hers with a jolt that shook her to her toes,
Anya experienced a moment of panic. Did she really
have a choice? Could she leave him? Her heart pounded
as he stepped up on the curb and wrapped her in a bear
hug, oblivious to the interested stares of passersby.

"I've missed you, love." His deep, husky voice warmed
her all the way through. She nodded, swallowing, pulling
away.

"I've missed you, too." It was no more than the truth.
She was alive again, just being with him. Her eyes misted
as she stepped up into the van and sat down in the big

seat. Watching him get in on the other side, she forced an answering smile to his flash of a grin. "You're early," she added, for something to say.

"Both of us. A good sign, maybe." That warm and possessive glance swept over her, and the grin brightened as she flushed. "Where's your car? I found a garage where we can leave it."

She told him, and then, while he drove to the right street, she explained about Marilee's coming in early, told him about her tour of the Dahlonega shops, chattered away about anything to hide how she felt. Then, in her own car as she followed him to the garage, she managed to calm herself. There would be a time in the next two days when she could talk sensibly. Confronting Brady now was impossible. You'd just cry, she told herself angrily. And then he'd put his arms around you and it would be all over.

At the garage, she climbed back into the van with a smile and headed for the curtained area in the back to change. She took her time about it, and when she made her way through the moving van in her jeans and yellow chamois shirt, she was easy and natural, the problem between them thrust firmly to the back of her mind.

Brady broke off his humming to sweep her with an approving look. "That's my girl." He reached out, engulfing her slim hand in his and holding it, gently stroking her wrist as he drove. "We'll be on private land this time. A friend of mine owns a stretch along a small river in the forest. Not as picturesque or rugged as the last place, but better for us."

Warmth ran from his hand, traveling up her arm and spreading insidiously through her. "Is it far?" she asked, sounding casually interested.

"We'll be there before dark." He looked at her again, a slow sweep of blue eyes that heightened the warmth into pulsing heat in her veins. She searched, rather frantically, for something more to say.

"Places to paint?" She sounded breathless. An unconscious smile curved her lips as she watched him, her eyes a soft leaf-green under the long dark lashes. She hadn't realized how hungry she had been for the sight and sound of him. His deep voice was as potent an aphrodisiac as his scent.

"I don't plan to paint," he said, surprising her. "I plan to concentrate on you." His hand tightened on hers as he added softly, "I can hardly wait to start."

Shakily, Anya withdrew her hand from his, kicked off her boots, and settled back, tucking her legs up, staring from the window without seeing a thing. Pure desire had flamed through her at his last words, pooling in her loins, expanding her breasts until tiny points pushed against the yellow chamois. Her ears were filled with the slow, heavy beat of her own heart. She closed her eyes, helplessly wondering how to fight herself. If the touch of Brady's hand and the sound of his voice could do this, what chance did she have?

The highway they traveled bordered the national forest for most of their ride, gently rolling and sometimes tortuous as it skirted foothills. It offered a continuous peaceful scene, miles of pines, and the varying colors of hardwoods that rose and fell in giant waves to blend into misty blue on the mountain peaks in the distance. Anya watched from her window until the peacefulness sank in, and then, as the van rolled along steadily, she went to the kitchenette and made sandwiches. Anything to keep busy and not think. There was a loaf of rye, thin corned beef, Swiss cheese, and a packet of sauerkraut, so she made Reuben sandwiches and put them away to be grilled when they stopped. Curiously unwilling to go back to her seat beside Brady, she stretched out on one of the benches. Minutes later, the van swerved, rumbled over gravel, and came to a halt. Anya sat up as Brady appeared in the opening.

"Ready to eat?" she asked brightly. "I can have coffee and sandwiches ready quickly."

He ignored the question, coming to sit beside her and

take her hands, looking at her squarely, the blue laser beam penetrating. "Want to tell me what's bothering you?"

How did he always *know?* "Not yet." She was breathless, half frightened and hating herself for it. "Maybe never. Let's have lunch." She tried to withdraw her hands, but he held them tightly.

"Anya..."

"No!" she said violently, her face flaring with color, her eyes suddenly angry. "I don't want to talk about it. Are you the only one with the right to keep silent?"

He stared at her for a long minute, then released her hands. "Of course not," he said quietly. "But when you want to talk, I'll listen."

Grilling the sandwiches, pouring coffee, Anya wondered dismally why she hadn't taken the opening. Was it because she was still a coward? Or because she couldn't quite believe that Brady's motives were as underhanded as they seemed? She hated to bring her thoughts to light— it would be as if she were accusing him. Sitting with him as they ate, she suddenly thought of a safe question.

"I've wondered about that man who came to your door that night," she said casually. "Since your place is so hidden, how did he find it?"

"He got directions from the state police," Brady said absently. "Why?"

Anya's eyes widened. "That's exactly the way he found Roger and Marilee's house," she said indignantly. "Either the police tell anyone anything they ask, or he must have a darned good connection with them. That's an invasion of..." She trailed off, watching Brady's face harden.

"So you recognized him. I had forgotten you'd met." Brady's voice was flat. "Why didn't you mention it before, Anya?"

She colored again, but kept her eyes on him. "I realized he must still be interested in the Bruner box, and I knew you didn't want to talk about that. I naturally supposed he was—was offering a bid."

Brady's rugged face relaxed. "I see." He smiled, a

flicker of humor in his eyes. "And you were right—I didn't want to talk about that. I still don't."

"I know you don't." She leaned forward, ready now to risk an argument. "But I don't know why. Is it because you don't trust me?"

The blue eyes didn't waver. "I'd trust you with my life," he said gravely, "and tell you anything that concerned only me. But if I talked to you about that damned box, I would have to lie. And I won't lie to you, Annie Anya."

She sat staring at him, knowing he had won. He had disarmed her completely with that enigmatic response. What he was saying was that the mystery of the music box concerned others besides himself, that if he told her the truth he would be violating a confidence. Whose? Morgan's? The man at the door? Or someone else? It could be anyone. And she didn't know a bit more than she had ever known, except that someone else was involved. It was very frustrating.

"I'll clean this up," she said abruptly, and reached for their plates, starting to rise.

"Not yet," Brady said, and pulled her down to sit beside him again. "I have a question myself." The blue eyes were penetrating again. "Do *you* trust *me?*"

"Of course I do," Anya said automatically, and then stared at him, knowing she had lied. "Wait," she added tremulously. "I—I'm not sure. I know I love you, but..." She stopped, wondering how to go on. Brady's face was a study in conflicting emotions. "I *want* to!" she burst out. "I'm trying, Brady!"

"I know," he said slowly, "and I guess I understand. You've been pulled into something you don't like and I can't explain. And it's my fault. I should have stayed away from you." He sat looking at her broodingly for a moment, and then took her in his arms, holding her tightly, pressing his face into her neck, "You will trust me, Anya. You'll learn." He raised his head and looked at her with a wry smile. "In the meantime, I'll settle for the love."

Anya's eyes were misting, her heart hurting. She had hated saying those things to Brady. She could feel the tension in him, sense how much he wanted her.

"The good news," she said shakily, "is that there's lots of it." She put her arms around him and kissed him, gently but lingeringly, feeling the jolt of desire that ran through them both.

"You shouldn't have done that," Brady said, only half teasing, and gently pushed her down on the bench, holding her there with his weight, taking her mouth this time with a passion that brought a humming moan of pleasure from her throat. A few minutes later, she surfaced to find her shirt half off, his hands busy with her bra.

"Brady, this isn't the place..."

"You're right." His hot breath was tantalizing in the cleft of her breasts. "We can't do this on a public road. Stop me."

Anya sighed and pushed him away, very slowly.

Around three o'clock, they came to a small settlement on the edge of the forest and turned to travel through, accompanied by stares from the few people on the street. The custom-made van, Anya had noticed, always attracted attention. Watching the heads turn, she realized the van's unusual appearance made it easy to trace, easy to recognize. Those men last weekend, she thought grimly, probably knew exactly who owned it. The thought was distinctly unpleasant, and she pushed it away, determined not to ruin this weekend.

On the north end of the little town, an unpaved road scrambled awkwardly upward. Shifting into low gear, Brady gave Anya's falling face an amused look.

"The price of privacy. Where roads are paved and straight, the whole world visits. This agony doesn't last long, love."

"That's nice to know." Anya grasped the hanging seat belt and held on as the van grumbled and bucked over ruts, rocks, and washouts. She looked at the narrowness of it and shuddered, hoping they wouldn't meet another car. The drop on the west side was deep and precipitous, though the hill leveled out quickly.

An ugly hill, she thought, the trees sparse and small, the underbrush scraggly. Compared to the rest of the forested land she had seen on the ride, it was desolate. But as it twisted and turned, she began to see a green valley in the distance. Looking back, watching the curves of the road appearing and disappearing behind them, she noted that another car could be seen occasionally, bumping and jouncing even more than the van.

"Someone else is willing to pay the price of privacy," she remarked. "I see a car back there."

Brady slowed, watching in the rearview mirror until the car appeared. It was loaded with camping equipment strapped on a luggage rack on top. "That's right," he said, sounding relieved. "There's a primitive camping area at the end of this road. We turn off long before that, and I'd forgotten it was there." He drove on, adding, "They won't be close enough to bother us, Annie Anya."

She was silent. Something in his sharp scrutiny of the car and the relief in his voice when he realized where it was going made her uneasy. Brady was a supremely confident man, used to a rough life, yet a following car had disturbed him. Watching, she saw his eyes return to the rearview mirror often before they came to the turnoff he mentioned. Then, once he had turned and was traveling west on a smoother and much more pleasant trail through the woods, he stopped.

"We'll just make sure," he said casually, "that they don't plan to trespass." He got out and walked back to a point where he could watch the hill road. He moved silently, tightly controlled, his back tense as he stood looking. Then, after a few minutes, he turned, smiling and relaxed, coming back toward her with his boots carelessly crunching through the leaves and brittle branches on the forest floor.

"They went on," he said as he climbed in again. "As well as I could tell, they didn't give this road a glance."

Anya was dying to ask why he was so concerned, what real difference it would make if they shared a whole valley with one other camping group. Instead, she smiled and murmured agreeably, while her thoughts raced on. Brady always wanted to be absolutely alone with her. He was forever snatching her away from the shop or out of crowds and hurrying her into his van or car. Even when he brought her home, he wouldn't come in ... no, that first time, bringing her home from the art show, he had come in for coffee with Roger and Marilee and had seemed to enjoy being with them—at least until Marilee had mentioned Morgan Whitcomb. She sighed. Everything went back to that damnable music box.

Angling southwest, the road they were on gradually sloped downward through big trees and open spaces until suddenly there was a wide swathe of golden grasses and a rocky shore along a shimmering sheet of blue, a slow-flowing river that reflected the blue October sky above. Anya looked at Brady and laughed.

"And you didn't bring your paints? It's lovely—so peaceful."

"That's the problem. People who buy mountain paintings want them wild and rugged. Exciting. This is calendar art—photographic." He smiled at her. "But safe. And exactly right for my present purposes. There's not a public road for miles." He reached for her and Anya opened the door on her side and leaped out, whirling to laugh up at his startled face.

"Oh, no, you don't. I don't fit between you and the steering wheel, remember? Anyway, I want to stretch my legs."

"Stretch them around me," Brady said seductively. "I'll be glad to help."

Anya swallowed more laughter. "Later," she said winningly, "I'll be a lot more flexible. Come show me your peaceable kingdom."

Brady's eyes showed plainly that he found the slender figure irresistible. Anya's dark hair glowed in the after-

noon sun; her huge eyes sparkled like jewels in her small
face. Hands on her hips in playful defiance, she stood
braced and waiting, her booted feet apart, slim legs and
hips outlined in the jeans, generous breasts thrusting
against the yellow chamois. He sighed and got out,
climbing awkwardly over her seat. Then, swinging one
powerful arm around her waist, he lifted her bodily into
the crook of his arm. She hung there like a sack of meal,
head down, arms and legs dangling, gasping for breath.
Ignoring her kicking feet, her hands frantically grasping
his thigh, her loud protests, he began carrying her toward
the shore.

"I ought to throw you in," he growled, "for making
me wait." He winced slightly. "And I will, dammit, if
you pinch me there again."

"I can't *breathe!*"

"Serves you right." He stopped, though, at the knee-
high grass, looking down at her dangling hair and red
face. "Had enough?"

Anya nodded her flopping head and then strangled on
laughter as he set her on her feet. She clung to him, her
forehead butted against his chest as she tried to get her
breath. Each gasping intake of air carried his scent—
warm male skin, the odor of wool, the faint drift of
woodsy soap he used. So familiar, so evocative of remembered ecstasy. As her breathing eased, her hands
slid slowly down from his wide shoulders and crept around
his waist. She swayed forward, pressing herself full length
against him, raising her head to look at him with eyes
darkened to a deep, glowing jade.

"It doesn't have to be a very long walk, darling."

Her parted lips were as irresistible as the rest of her.
Brady claimed them with a bruising kiss, his arms going
around in a crushing embrace. His insistent tongue probed
the softness of her mouth hungrily, his hands searched
down to grasp her small, rounded buttocks and fit her
tightly to his loins.

"Br-Bra-a-ady..." Started as a protest, the small,
broken sound ended in an erotic moan as Anya surren-

dered to the kiss, to the feeling of his strong body hot against her. Burning, she felt him tremble and knew that he, too, was on the ragged edge of control, that the slightest nudge might send them both hurtling into the mindless world of overpowering desire. But her feminine desire to tease him a little, to see how far she could go before he rebelled, pushed her into a subtle movement. Imperceptibly, she tilted her hips, widened her thighs slightly, and brushed slowly, luxuriously, across his bulging loins. Her own body flamed as she heard the deep sound in his chest, felt the jolt that ran through him.

"That did it," Brady said roughly, and pulled her down with him into the bending sun-golden grass, muffling her startled, half-frightened cry with his panting mouth, threw a taut leg over her twisting thighs to subdue them. "You really asked for this, you know."

"We—we walked far enough," Anya gasped, pushing frantically at his rock-hard chest. "I'm ready to g-go back." She fought his hands, which seemed to be all over her, taking her clothes apart, pushing up her shirt, loosening her jeans. His mouth moved to an unfettered breast, shining golden in the sun, and captured the rosy tip and rolled it with a rough tongue.

"Oh, Lord..." Anya whimpered, closing her eyes. She could feel her disobedient body arch, pressing the breast tighter to his mouth, then felt the rough stems of grass against her bare skin as he pushed her jeans down, his hands rough but efficient, rolling her back and forth to free the cloth. "Oh, please, Brady..."

His hands and mouth left her. There was nothing touching her at all but the sun and a drift of cool air, the rasping roughness of the grass beneath her. She opened her eyes and saw him hovering over her, big and dark, silhouetted in a dazzling aureole of sunlight against the blue sky.

"I can't," he said, in a tone of complete frustration. "You look too damned uncomfortable." He ran a hand over the sleek skin of her hip, and sighed. "Silk like this needs something soft under it, not *this*." He grabbed a handful of the tough, stiff stems and tossed it away, reaching for her hand. "Come on, love, I guess you win."

She had never loved him more. The corners of her mouth quivered and tilted upward. "Your shirt is soft," she murmured, and watched the blue eyes widen, the creases in his cheeks deepen with a slow smile. Then he was sitting back, hastily unbuttoning his shirt.

"I feel like Eve," she sighed a while later, sliding her arms around his neck. His shirt beneath her was still warm from his body, and the sight of them coming together, skin glistening in the sun, made her breathless. His hair-roughened, muscular frame, the sheer virility of his taut, fully aroused loins as he swung between her slender thighs were incredibly erotic. Desire flowed through her in an irresistible tide. She was trembling with it, her hands urging, sliding down to the hard buttocks to press him toward her as she lifted her hips invitingly.

"If Eve had looked like you," Brady said thickly, "she wouldn't have needed an apple." He took her with a rush, driving deep, pinning her down in purely instinctive male domination. Then, easing, feeling her long legs wrap around his, her body rippling beneath him, he leaned forward and kissed her sunlit face, touching the closed eyes and flushed cheeks, taking the soft mouth tenderly. "Ah, Annie Anya, how I love you . . ."

Behind her closed eyes, the sun swung down and lifted them both, swung up again, carrying them into the fiery bliss of love. There was no time but this.

Chapter 12

WANDERING NORTH ALONG the placid, smooth-running river in early morning, Brady showed Anya a bend where swirling eddies formed pools and trout gathered. Wearing oversized waders, Anya struggled with the intricacies of a fly rod and finally gave up, taking off the waders in favor of sitting on the bank and applauding as Brady caught three fat rainbows.

"We'll grill them for dinner," he said. "They're the other thing I know how to cook."

Anya thought how carelessly happy he looked. And how seldom he looked that way. Walking back to the van at noon, she thought of their first days together, when he'd seemed so easy and free. Marilee's innocent mention of Morgan Whitcomb had changed that. Anya looked along the gentle slopes of the valley and the foothills rising protectively around them and wished they could stay hidden forever from problems.

"I'm going to hate leaving here," she said.

Brady laughed, sweeping an arm around her, hugging her to him. "I'm winning. You'll be a wilderness nut in no time. Later, we'll do a lot of camping."

Later. When what he had to do was over. When all the loose ends were tied up. She took a chance on a question. "When will that be?"

He looked away, his face tightening again. "I don't know, Annie Anya. It's taking longer than I thought."

For the first time, he sounded as if he wasn't in control of what was going on. That scared her. She stopped, and he stopped with her, looking at her inquiringly.

"I won't ask you what the problem is," she said defensively, "because I know you won't tell me. But—are *you* in danger?"

Brady smiled, shifting the fishing equipment from one shoulder to the other, smiling down at her indulgently. "Me? Absolutely not. Does that help?"

"You know it does." Weak with relief, she walked on. She didn't doubt him, and suddenly the sun was warmer, the breeze fresher, the beauty around them brighter. "I *have* wondered," she confessed. "You've been so cautious."

"Evidently," Brady said grimly, "not cautious enough." He had stopped again, his head turned toward the eastern hills, his blue eyes narrowing. "We have a visitor," he added, his voice flat. Then, curtly, he said, "Keep going, Anya. Don't run, but go straight to the van and get in. Wait there for me."

"What? *Why?*" Confused, frightened by his tone, she followed his gaze to the edge of the woods and saw nothing. "I don't see—"

"*Go.*"

She went. The van was now only a hundred yards away, and she tracked a straight line to it. But it still seemed like miles. She glanced over her shoulder once and saw a man emerging from the woods, walking casually through the high grass and down to Brady. Then, inside the van and watching from a window, Anya's heart steadied. They were talking, that was all. The man, who was almost as tall as Brady and considerably heavier, had his head thrown back, laughing. Just someone Brady hadn't wanted her to meet, with talk he hadn't wanted her to hear. Probably something to do with his problem, his secrets. Damn! He could have just said so! Why yell at her, scare her to death? She turned away and went to the back of the van to wash her face. She was brushing her hair when she heard the door slam in the front and the engine start.

"Anya!"

She went forward, staggering as the van backed up and then leaped ahead. "What in the world . . . ?" The seat where she usually sat was full of fishing equipment and the creel that held the trout, thrown there haphazardly. Brady was jockeying the van around to head up the trail. "We're leaving?"

"Stay in back," Brady said harshly, "and keep out of sight. I mean it."

She clung to the back of his seat, angry again. "Tell me what's going on! What are we running from?"

Slowing, looked at her with fury in his rough face, Brady answered in a roar. "Will you do as I say, or do I have to come back there and tie you down?"

Anya turned, tears of mixed rage and fear clouding her vision, and went back, hanging on as the van sped up the trail, swerving constantly as it wound around trees. She half fell on a bench and clung, watching the forest spin by and wondering if Brady had gone completely crazy. As mountain trails went, this one wasn't too bad, but it was hardly a turnpike. It wasn't *safe*. She closed her eyes, breathing deeply, and tried to calm herself. At least when he came to that road over the hill, he would *have* to slow down.

He didn't. The van leaned precariously on the turn, went roaring upward, crashing over small rocks, swerving to the outside edge of the road to avoid bigger ones. Dipping and jouncing in washouts, winding around the tortuous curves, the van seemed to hover continually on the verge of destruction. The noise inside was almost as frightening as the sheer drop outside. Cabinets reverberated with the crash of pans and dishes, the van body clanged as it bucked over rocks, the engine clattered and roared.

He *is* crazy, Anya thought, terrified, and leaned forward, clinging to the bolted-down table, and stared toward the front seats. All she could see was a shoulder and a big hand on the gearshift. The hand moved, shifting smoothly, as steady as ever. They were nearing the top of the long hill; she could see it ahead. Smoother, without so many rocks.

There was a new noise, a noise like a swarm of angry bees, growing louder. Behind them. Anya twisted on the bench, looking back, feeling her heart jump crazily and lodge in her throat. Coming around the bend were a dozen or so men on weird, fat-wheeled vehicles that leaped over the rocks and raced through the washouts as if they weren't there. She gasped as four of them turned off and went shooting up the steep slope of the hill, then came tearing through the underbrush and sparse trees above the road, the men looking down, yelling and waving at Brady to stop.

Anya cowered back, but not before she saw the faces beneath the padded helmets they wore. Padded helmets like the river runners wore. The gang. The wild bunch Brady had told her about. They were close now, passing the van, shouting. She heard one of them plainly—"Stop or bust up, Durant!"—followed by a crazy burst of laughter.

The men drew in, dropping down into the road as the hill flattened before the descent. They wove back and forth in front, sped along the sides, whooping and laughing. If anything, the van went faster, tilting as the downward slope began. Anya stifled a scream as a gun went off, and then heard with horror a fusillade of gunshots. She flung herself forward across the table, looking. He wasn't hurt. The hand still moved steadily; the shoulder was straight. From this angle, she could see the side of Brady's head, the set jaw. She slid back down on the bench, burying her face in her hands, holding back tears.

It was some minutes before she realized that the sound of gunshots had stopped, and the sound of the snarling, buzzing vehicles was fading in the distance. She sat up and looked out, seeing through blurred eyes that the outskirts of the little highway settlement were just ahead. The van slowed and stopped, and Brady's tall figure appeared in the opening.

Anya scrambled around the table and fell into his arms. "Oh, thank God! I thought we'd both be killed!"

"I'm sorry, love. I didn't have time to explain. If they'd caught me before the top of the hill, I might have had to hit one of them to get through. It's all right now."

"But they *shot* at you!" She was struggling with tears.

"They shot into the air," Brady said gently. "They don't want to hurt me, they just want to talk. Please, Anya, calm down. It isn't that bad."

She pulled away from him, grabbing a paper towel, scrubbing at her face like a child. "Then, why scare me to death? Why not just talk to them?" Anger was drying her tears. "You could have killed us both!"

"I didn't want them to see you," Brady said quietly. "They know I have a woman with me, but they haven't seen your face. I don't want them to know who you are."

She turned and looked at him, surprised. "Why not? Anyway, they know who I am—at least I think one of them does..." She stopped, startled as his hands shot out and grasped her arms.

"What do you mean? How could they know?"

Anya stared at him, surprised by the intensity of his tone. "I don't know—I only know I recognized one of them, and I'm sure he knows me. He might have even seen me getting into the van in Dahlonega."

Brady groaned, turning her toward the bench. "All right, Anya, you'd better sit down and tell me all of it."

She told him about the man who had been watching her in Dahlonega, who had turned away when he knew she saw him. "He went across the street, but he didn't go far. Then you came along and picked me up."

"I wish you'd mentioned it at the time," Brady said grimly.

"It didn't seem important—until I saw him on one of those crazy motor things."

"ATV's."

"What?"

"All Terrain Vehicles," Brady said impatiently. "Hell,

it doesn't matter. You sure it was the same man?"

She nodded. "I'm sure. I think I've seen him in the shop, too." She jumped as Brady slapped the top of the table with the flat of his hand.

"Morgan! I should have known."

Anya stared at his stiff, angry face. "What do you mean by that?"

"I mean," Brady said harshly, "that Morgan has told them to keep an eye on you. We're going to Atlanta."

Anya's face was pale now. "Those men," she said, and swallowed. "They are—*them*, aren't they? The men who play games."

"They're a bunch of baboons," Brady said shortly, and got up. "Forget them. I'll get this rig in shape." He went forward and came back with the fishing equipment, shoved the trout in the refrigerator, and put the rest away. His boots crunched on broken glass and he leaned down, picking up the remains of wineglasses jolted from the cabinet above. His creased face was tight and stern, softening only as he put his arms around Anya again.

"I gave you a wild, rough ride, love, but maybe it was worth it. Those men want something from me, and they've got odd ways of persuasion. Come on up front and relax. It's a long trip."

Anya pulled away. "No. I want to change. Just drive carefully for a few minutes." She left him, going quickly toward the rear of the van, pulling the curtain across. Her heart beat painfully; she felt shocked and unsure. Whatever Brady was mixed up in, something was very, very wrong. She understood too well what he had meant— the odd ways of persuasion would have involved *her*.

The van was rolling smoothly on the highway when Anya curled up in her seat. She was wearing narrow black slacks, a white silk blouse, and the bulky emerald sweater. Her hair shone mahogany from brushing, and her lips and cheeks had a light touch of color. Faint smudges around her eyes added to the delicacy of her face. Brady gave her a sweeping, all-inclusive glance that didn't miss the firm set of the small jaw.

"Beautiful," he said, "but I think I prefer Eve."

"Eve had a very short life," Anya said dismissively. She was in no mood for banter. "Brady, if I'm involved in this, I have a right to know what's going on."

"You're not involved," he said calmly, "and I'm going to see that everyone understands that. Just forget it."

Anya looked away. In one short period of time, she had been terrified, yelled at, and had found out someone had been trailing her. She felt very much involved. "I suppose," she said carefully, "that you aren't going to report them this time, either."

Brady gave an impatient grunt. "Report them for what? Riding around a hill on ATV's? Whooping? Shooting into the air? Be sensible, darling."

Anya's temper flew away. "I am, dammit! I'm looking out for myself! I want to know why that man was watching me—why, suddenly, I'm so important to some—some *criminals*. I want you to tell me, Brady, just what game they're playing now, and what part you have in it."

In some mysterious way, her temper calmed him. "At this point," he said mildly, "the less you know, the better. Trust me."

She stared at him, the fury in her green eyes slowly burning down, changing to bleak despair. "I wish I could," she said finally, flatly, and leaned back, setting her jaw and turning her face to the window.

The suburb where the Whitcombs lived was predictably lush, the homes imposing, the grounds around them spacious and well landscaped. The Whitcomb house was neoclassic in the best southern tradition—tall white Grecian columns and a deep, wide veranda with double doors that were opened by a smiling manservant when Brady knocked.

They waited in a wide marble-floored foyer while the manservant went to find Paul Whitcomb. Mrs. Whitcomb, he had informed them, was not at home. Glancing

around as they waited, Anya thought the house handsome
but hardly what she would have expected Morgan to
choose. The few pieces of furniture she could see were
dark and massive, the staircase uncompromisingly heavy
and straight, the steps covered with dark turkey-red car-
peting that was lush but sober. Morgan was always so
light, so full of gaiety...

"Brady. Nice of you to drop in. And Mrs. Meredith!
Wonderful to see you again." Whit's lined face was genial
as he hurried toward them from the back of the hall.
"Come into the library for a drink. Morgan will be disappointed that she didn't see you..."

Seated in the library while Whit poured bourbon for
Brady and himself, a glass of Perrier for Anya, Brady
asked casually when Morgan would be home.

"Heaven knows," Whit said cheerfully, proffering the
drinks and sitting down. "She's gone on one of what she
calls her 'weekend retreats.' I suppose she needs them—
she's usually so active, you know. And she's been very
upset..." He stopped, looking at Brady. "I'm sure she's
told you that someone stole her favorite toy—that antique music box?" It was a question, and Brady answered
it.

"No, she didn't," he said carefully, and set his glass
down. "When?"

"Oh, a couple of weeks ago, I think. A smart thief—
in and out without tripping the alarm, and I have a good
system. Anyway, she's been up in the air and irritable
ever since, and frankly, I'm glad she decided to go. She
always comes back in a good humor."

Anya sipped her Perrier and watched the white-haired
old man with a wry sympathy. Brady picked up his glass
again, drained it, and refused another.

"Where does she go?" he asked Whit.

"I don't know," Whit answered carelessly. "One of
the health farms, I suppose. More Perrier, Mrs. Meredith?"

Brady stood up. "We only stopped in for a minute,
Whit. Thanks, anyway."

In the van, Brady was morose. "Weekend retreats," he said savagely, driving away. "She lied to me about breaking off with that gang. And lied to Whit about the music box. I wonder if she ever tells the truth."

Anya glanced at him. Brady didn't lie. He simply wouldn't answer questions. "Maybe," she volunteered, "she's up at that camp near the valley."

"She's with some of them," Brady said, "but not those. She would never have missed going along on the chase."

Anya's mouth dropped open. "Morgan? On one of those—those ATV's?"

"Morgan rides like the demon she is," Brady answered sardonically. "One of the best." He looked ahead, gradually easing out into a long line of traffic leaving the city. "This looks like a long trip, darling."

Anya's mind flashed back to the gold earring on the floor of the van. "Maybe she's the one who searched the van," she said slowly. "Remember the earring you found? It wasn't mine."

"It could have been hers," Brady agreed, and looked at Anya curiously. "Why didn't you mention it before?"

Anya blushed. "Well, I didn't exactly think of it as—as criminal evidence. I thought..."

Brady grinned, his tired face brightening. "You thought some other woman had been sleeping there?" He reached out, taking her hand, caressing the wrist with his thumb. "I haven't been a monk, Anya, but there's been no other woman in my van."

Anya wished she hadn't mentioned it. What difference did it make which one of his "friends" had searched the van? She turned her face to the window, her eyes blurring. His hand was so warm, so strong, so enticing—but what was in his mind? She thought of Whit, deliberately blind to what he didn't want to see. He loved Morgan, so he shut his eyes. Maybe I've been doing that, she thought painfully. I've got to get away—far enough away to *think*. Someplace where I can't see him and he can't touch me. Tomorrow, or the next day...so far, she couldn't even pull her hand from his.

"This traffic is terrible," she said, only for something to break the silence. "It'll take a long time to get to Dahlonega."

"We aren't going to Dahlonega." Brady still wore a faint smile. "There's only one place I want to be tonight. We're going home."

It took her a moment to understand. "Your house?"

"Our house," he said, his hand tightening, and drove on.

Chapter 13

ANYA AWOKE TO the peaceful silence of the dense forest that surrounded Brady's house. He had left the van. She could see his moon-silvered figure moving up the steps to the darkened house. In a moment, lights sprang on and Brady reappeared, coming toward her with his long, silent stride, his rugged features accented by the light pouring down from a full moon in a clear sky.

"I'll get your suitcase, Annie Anya. We're home." Stepping in, he smiled down at her tousled hair and sleepy face, reached to stroke a tangled strand from her smooth forehead. "One hell of a day, wasn't it? But it's over."

Climbing out, Anya stood still with a feeling of immense relief. Cold, filled with the scent of pines, the air was clean and crisp. The broad bulk of the house, shining with welcoming light, offered warmth and safety.

"Peaceful," she said as Brady came up with her bag. Putting an arm around her, leading her to the steps, Brady hugged her.

"Let's keep it that way." Inside the door, he put her bag on the stairs and turned on more lights. "Sandwiches and coffee, I think. But first..." He strode to the niche beneath the stairs and neatly extracted the telephone wire from the wall. "I'm tired of other people. Tonight is for us."

The last night for us, Anya thought. Looking at the relief in his tired face, the warmth in the blue, blue eyes, she hadn't the courage to tell him. In a way, she thought sadly, I am no more honest with him than he is with me.

She turned away, taking off her sweater, dropping it on the gray tweed couch.

"I'll make the sandwiches," she said, and headed for the kitchen. She was washing her hands at the sink when Brady put his arms around her from behind and rested his chin on her shoulder.

"I *am* hungry for food, love."

Remembering, Anya felt a bubble of irrepressible laughter rising in her throat, followed closely by a sob. She tried to swallow both, twisting in his arms, reaching for a towel. She was immediately pinned against the yellow counter, Brady's arms going around her, his mouth on hers. His kiss was as potent as ever, alive with passionate tenderness. She yielded helplessly, putting her arms around him, holding him close while the familiar fire ran through her veins. But slow tears pushed out beneath her dark lashes and ran down her cheeks.

Brady leaned back, brushing the tears away. "Ah, darling, it's hit you hard, hasn't it? I'm sorry. I promise you, it won't happen again."

He looked so contrite, so sincere, so—so lovable. She wanted to pull the rough head down, kiss him, and tell him everything was all right. But everything *wasn't* all right. She moved, wiping her eyes and forcing a smile.

"I'm just tired, Brady. Let's get the coffee perking." If only he had taken her back to the Postons' house. There, she could have told him. Getting sandwich fixings from the refrigerator, she thought how simple it would have been. She could see herself standing on the porch, saying firmly that she had had enough—saying it would never work for them. Saying good-bye. *Good-bye.*

"Let me finish that." Brady was taking the slabs of ham, the cheese, and the lettuce away from her, pushing her down on a kitchen stool. "You're crying again." He bent, kissing a tear from her cheek. "It's over, Anya. All over, for you."

She wished she dared tell him how true that was. All over. Except for tonight. She sat there quietly, watching his hands, so quick and deft as he filled and sliced sandwiches. In the bright lights of the kitchen, he looked older, the lines in his face deeper. But there was nothing about him, from the top of his tumbled hair to the bottom of his well-worn boots, that she didn't love. She loved all of him. Wanted all of him, even if only for one more night. There would be time enough afterward for crying.

Later, going up the stairs, she slipped an arm around his waist. "I'm very tired," she confided, "but a shower might help, don't you think?"

Brady's real grin showed up for the first time since noon. "I think it might do us both a world of good. Just don't ask me to think while we're in there together."

That sounded right. Don't think, just feel. In the shower, she insisted on taking a big luffa sponge to his back, massaging the thick muscles, working down to his narrow flanks, turning the long legs into columns of foam.

The misty image of the slender woman in the chrome walls was diligent but gentle; the misty image of the tall man became rapidly aroused. Turning him so the water flooded away the foam on his back, Anya tossed aside the sponge and began on his chest with her palms, spreading soap with small, kneading circles. She ignored his condition, her water-starred lashes fringing huge emerald eyes with an innocent expression, her satiny belly brushing against him casually.

It was bittersweet to feel Brady's powerful body tremble beneath her touch and know it was for the last time. Anya's throat was tight as she moved lower, prolonging her caressing strokes as she reached his loins. She felt the involuntary movement, heard his indrawn breath, and then, beginning to tremble herself, her own loins aching with desire, she dropped to her knees and began on his legs, her slim hands circling and kneading the strong, corded thighs.

Brady's hands grasped her and pulled her to her feet, dragged her under the cascading water, and held her while the soapy foam she had coated him with flowed away.

"What happened to that shy little housewife," he asked hoarsely, "who knew nothing about making love?" Taking the soap, he bathed her already throbbing body, his big hands wickedly skillful. When he had her gasping, wildly offering herself for more, he smiled and turned the water off.

"Now," he said, "I'll dry you."

It was impossible to say which was the more tantalizing, the bath or the way Brady wielded the warm, thick towel. Anya snatched a towel and tried to reciprocate. They tangled, fought, laughed, and ended in a damp, clinging embrace in bed, surging together into an instant joining, an incredible, soaring consummation. A Fourth of July, with bursting rockets and exploding stars.

"Witch," Brady murmured afterward, and lifted her over him, looking up at her dazed, sensuous face. "A soft, curvy witch with shiny green eyes. The real Anya." He eased her down on his chest and hugged her. "Didn't I tell you what she'd be like? Wild, passionate..."

"And brave," Anya finished, a wry note in her still-breathless voice. "So, I'm not brave, darling. You must have found that out today."

He was silent, stroking her back, kneading the rounded buttocks. "Unknown danger frightens anyone," he said finally. "You have to see the face of an enemy before you find courage."

Anya raised her head and looked at him, half laughing. "Brady Durant, philosopher," she teased, then laid her cheek back down in his neck. "It sounds good," she added, half shamed. "I wish I could believe it. But I think I'm a natural-born coward. I don't even want to see danger."

"You won't, again," Brady said. "I'll see to that." He was rearranging her pliant body, shifting her until she lay full length on top of him, her long legs meshing with his, her full breasts crushed into the pelt of hair on his chest. There was, she noted, a certain male liveliness occurring beneath her, an uncertain note in his voice as he added, "Are you sleepy, love?"

Anya gave an exaggerated yawn. "I could stay awake," she said carelessly, "if it became necessary. Is it necessary?"

Brady rolled, ending with her flat on her back and his bending head seeking the tip of a full breast. "It's necessary," he muttered. "I need tonight to remember."

Beginning a slow caressing, feeling the deep stir of new desire, Anya thought vaguely that it was strange that he had said it that way. As if he knew they were parting.

They went to sleep in the first faint light of dawn and awoke to a bright, cold day at noon. Reluctantly.

"If I weren't starving," Brady groaned, burrowing against her warmth, "I'd stay here all day. Can you cook, Annie Anya?"

Anya smiled to herself and slid from bed, stretching luxuriously, unconcerned by her nakedness. "Yes. Hey, it's *cold!*" She ran to the closet and found a short, gold velour robe and wrapped it around herself, tying it tightly. "I'll fix something to eat while you dress."

Still huddled in blankets, Brady gave her a charming grin. "Turn up the thermostat on your way, darling. It's at the head of the stairs." He laughed as she slanted a derisive green glance at him. "It's nice to have such a beautiful woman to wait on me."

Playing house. Husband and dutiful wife. The words came to Anya's mind as she paused, reset the thermostat, and then pattered down the stairs in her bare feet. Well, why not? For a few hours more, she could act out the dream and then close the book on the last chapter. A lovely interlude between her dull life with Tom and the new life in New York. A new life in which she would have to subsist on these memories for a long, long time . . .

Taking eggs and bacon from the refrigerator, running a practiced eye over the contents of the cabinets, she set about preparing a breakfast to fill that rangy frame. She would think about closing the book when the time came to close it. Right now, she was cooking.

Twenty minutes later, Brady ran an incredulous gaze over the crisp bacon, scrambled eggs, stack of pancakes, and pitcher of warm, butter-laced honey. He sat down, looking up at Anya's flushed, relaxed face as she poured his coffee.

"Who makes breakfast like this these days?"

"Me," Anya said ungrammatically, and sat down to a scrambled egg and piece of rye toast. "I love to cook. It's my only talent. Now, eat, before it gets cold."

Halfway through, Brady gave her a look of deep respect. "It's not talent, Anya. It's pure genius. Why didn't you tell me?"

"You didn't ask." She laughed at the look he gave her as he reached for another pancake. "Anyway, I loved your steaks." She sat watching him with dreaming eyes, toying with her own food, sipping coffee. Brady would have loved her lamb ragout, her Dutch apple pie.

"I'll get fat," he murmured, spearing the last pancake. "I don't think I'll even fight it."

Not from one breakfast, you won't. The thought sobered her. She rose and took her plate and cup to the kitchen. Coming back, she poured him the last cup of coffee.

"You can put the dishes in the dishwasher," she said, and hesitated. "I had forgotten that I left my car in Dahlonega. We'll have to leave a little earlier." She slipped around the silvery screen and went quickly to the stairs.

She *had* forgotten, and now her plans were tangled. She had pictured the farewell so clearly—saying it all quick and fast on the Postons' porch. Then slipping inside, closing the door. Her soft mouth twisted as she ran up the stairs. Anya Meredith, coward. But, dammit, it was about the only way she could bear to do it! Now, she faced trying to tell him in the van, or hastily on a street corner while she shifted from the van to her car. Awkward, impossible—but it had to be done.

She took a shower, spending a long time in it. The black slacks were still in a crumpled pile on the floor, so she put on a fresh pair of jeans and the cream turtleneck sweater. Then she packed and repacked her suitcase until she realized she was simply putting off the moment when she had to face Brady with the truth. Then she fastened the bag and picked it up, forcing her feet to carry her through the door and down the stairs.

Brady had built a small fire in the fireplace and was standing there, brooding and watching the flames. He looked up as she came down and went silently to meet her. He put her suitcase by the entrance door and turned back, taking her arm and leading her to the couch in front of the fire.

"Before we go, there's something I have to say," he said. "I've been putting it off since last night." He pulled her down on the couch and put an arm around her. "I'd like to put it off forever, but I can't. Will you try to understand?"

Anya looked at his somber face. If Brady was going to confess something she didn't want to hear, then—then she didn't want to hear it! She looked away. "You don't have to tell me anything—not now."

Brady smiled faintly. "Yes, I do. You know I love you, Anya. And I think you know that I want you in my life permanently." He stopped, cocking an eye at her when she made a small, demurring sound. "You do know that, love."

"Maybe," she said weakly, "but I don't agree with it."

"You will," he said, pulling her closer. "But that's beside the point. The point is that I have to stop seeing you for a while."

Jolted, Anya stared at the fire, struggling with a feeling of disbelief and an insane desire to argue. Brady had just saved her the agony of telling him good-bye, and she should be grateful. How could it hurt so much?

"All right," she said numbly, "if that's what you want."

"You know it's not what I want," he said gently. "It's the way it has to be. And that's not all. I want you to leave Helen. You've been talking about going to New York, and that's as good a place as any. I want you to go tonight. Or at least by tomorrow." He stood, pulling her up into his arms, holding her tightly. "Will you do it, love? Just go, without any questions? It's important to me."

She felt stiff and awkward in his arms. She kept her face averted, her hands pressed to his chest. He had never been more of a stranger than he was right now. Why should she ask questions? He had described exactly what she had intended to do, and all she had to do now was agree.

"I will," she said slowly. "I'm sure it's for the best." She looked up, seeing the strain in the blue eyes, the tension in the craggy face. "And I won't ask any questions."

"Ah, Anya..." He bent his head to kiss her, and she moved away quickly.

"Don't." Picking up her handbag, she refused to look at him; she knew he'd see the agony in her eyes. "It won't make it any easier, Brady. Let's go. I'll need time to—to make arrangements."

He was looking puzzled and hurt. "It isn't forever, Anya. Only long enough to clear up a problem and—"

"Tie up the loose ends," she finished for him, and forced a smile. There were too many loose ends. All those wild, lawless men. Morgan. And, behind it all, that stupid music box and the tall, quiet man who wanted it. Sometimes she thought he was the most dangerous of all. Anya watched Brady put a heavy screen in front of the dying fire and wondered if his life was always so complicated.

In the van, Brady went on with his plans for her. "Don't try to find anything permanent in New York, Anya. It won't be worthwhile. Send your address to Marilee when you're settled and I'll get it from her."

Watching his tense, stern face, Anya agreed to everything. She knew she wouldn't do as he said; she thought he probably didn't expect her to. She was one extra complication in a complicated life, and one he could do without. She didn't fit in.

Because it was Sunday, there was no one but the watchman at the garage. He opened the big door and let them into the cavernous, dark interior. "Just slam it shut," he told Brady. "The lock will catch." He wandered away, yawning.

"There must not be much crime in Dahlonega," Brady commented, carrying in Anya's suitcase to put it in her car. He smiled, but the smile didn't reach his eyes. He tossed the bag in and took her in his arms, ignoring her resistance. "Maybe it doesn't make it easier," he said huskily, "but I can't leave you without it."

His kiss was insistent, demanding, warmly possessive. Anya's unwilling mouth softened in spite of her; her stiff body melted and clung. She was weak and close to tears when she finally broke away and slid behind the wheel of her car.

"Good luck," she said shakily, "in whatever it is you're trying to do. And good-bye." The word came out with finality.

Brady was leaning on the car, his long fingers hooked over the window, his eyes their deepest blue. "Not really good-bye, Annie Anya. It never will be."

Another moment, Anya thought despairingly, and I'll be bawling like a baby. She turned the key and gunned the engine into a roar that reverberated hollowly in the garage. "Well, it still runs," she said, falsely bright. "I'll be off."

"Wait. I nearly forgot..." Reaching into his pocket, Brady handed her a slip of paper. "If—well, in an emergency, call this number. They'll find me. And be careful, love. I couldn't stand to lose you now."

The words reminded her of the first night they had spent by the wild river, the night she had felt so free.

She didn't trust herself to speak as she took the paper and shoved it deep into a pocket of her jeans. She gave him what she hoped was a cheerful nod and drove out of the dark garage into the bright afternoon sun, blinking back tears, narrowly missing the rear of his van. Be careful, indeed. There ought to be a law against driving with a broken heart.

Chapter 14

ARGUING WITH MARILEE that night wasn't easy. Anya couldn't explain. All she could do was repeat, "Brady and I are in agreement—I should leave."

"Then you're both crazy," Marilee said finally. "If I've ever seen two people in love..."

"Oh, *please!*"

Marilee's mouth closed with a snap. Rising, she began to clear the dinner table. "Well," she said crossly, "if you can stay until noon tomorrow, it will give me a chance to hire someone else."

"I can do that," Anya assented tiredly. Any delay was frustrating, but she owed Marilee, and staying one more morning with the twins wouldn't kill her. She forced a smile. "I'll be glad to, Marilee. I can use the rest."

By morning, Anya was hollow-eyed with exhaustion. She hadn't slept at all, only wrestled with a rebellious heart. She hated leaving Brady. Forcing herself, she brought coffee to her bedroom and packed, keeping out the gray slacks, a silk shirt, and the red woolly coat. It was cold; beautiful weather without a cloud in the sky. It would have suited her better if the sky had been gray, with a dismal rain falling.

By ten-thirty, her bags were packed and she was ready to leave. Betty Sue had taken the twins and dogs for a walk. Now Anya could hear them returning, making cheerful sounds in their various ways. She had no desire to join them. She sat on the windowsill, gazing out at the immense forest and wondering when, if ever, those fugitives would be caught and Marilee could relax. She was rising from the sill and thinking of trying to take a nap when the sound of a diesel jolted her heart. She stared from the window until the top of a van appeared. White, rusty, with a sign on the side that read: KROGER'S PLUMBING CO. She turned away as the truck pulled up and stopped. She really should rest.

"Annie Anya?" Betty Sue, downstairs. Anya sighed and went to the open door.

"Yes?"

"The men from Kroger's Plumbing are here to fix the furnace. Shall I let them in?" Betty Sue was always careful.

"What's wrong with the furnace?"

"Nothing. They say Mr. Poston just wants it cleaned out good and checked before hard winter sets in."

"Oh. Well, of course, let them in." Anya stood there, listening to the heavy bolt slide back, the keys jangling, and thought what a bother it all was. Then she sighed and headed for the bed. Lying down, stretching, she promised herself not to think of Brady...

Downstairs, Betty Sue screamed, shattering the air with the sound of sheer terror, sliced into silence by a rough command.

"Knock that off!"

For an instant, Anya was paralyzed, staring at the ceiling. Then she was off the bed, scrambling for the stairs, stopping halfway down and staring at a horrifying tableau. A man in the hall was pointing a pistol at Betty Sue; behind Betty Sue was a motionless mass of blond curls and quivering brown-and-white fur—the twins and the beagles. It was a play, the actors waiting for their cues. Not real.

The man looked up at her and motioned with the pistol. Her cue. Anya drew air into starved lungs and forced her feet down steps until she reached the bottom. Part of her mind told her the man wore khaki work clothes, was overweight with a heavy, belligerent-looking face. Another part of her mind frantically assured her that he wasn't there. He couldn't be.

"I find nothing threatening." A disembodied voice.

Anya started violently. Another man had appeared, silent and quick, coming from the back of the house. He was carrying a weapon like no other weapon Anya had ever seen. Boxlike and black with strapped bullets hanging from it. It looked murderous. The man looked murderous. Like a coiled snake, dark and slim, with eyes as flat and black as his gun. He stared back at her calmly.

"You are Brady Durant's woman?" His voice was soft and oddly cadenced, the rhythm clearly foreign. *Foreign!*

Reality burst forth in Anya's mind. These men were danger. They were death. *They liked hostages*. And she, she herself, had told Betty Sue to let them in. She moved across to stand between Betty Sue and the gun.

"Yes, I am Brady Durant's woman." She said it firmly, even with a kind of relief. If they wanted her, perhaps they would let the others go. "What do you want from me?"

The man's thin lips stretched meaninglessly. "At the moment, patience." He ran lightly up the stairs. Anya heard doors open and close and knew he was searching the place. She waited, listening. Behind her, there was only Betty Sue's rasping breath. Anya dared to glance around, seeing the twins crouched on the floor, their brown eyes wide and terrified. Each had a plump arm around a beagle, each had a thumb in her mouth. They knew; how did they know? Anya swallowed a lump in her throat. So little, so frightened.

"There is no danger in the house, Harry." The dark man's rhythmic words were the only sound he made coming down the stairs. The heavy man relaxed and grinned, turning to the door.

"My partner wants to be in on this," he said. "Hold the fort." His voice was clearly American.

The slim man looked at Anya, stretching his lips again.

"Send your maid and her charges upstairs. Small children annoy me."

Betty Sue didn't wait to be told. She whirled and grasped the dogs, picking them up, shooing the twins ahead of her, her voice squeaking with fright as she urged them to hurry. For once, Susan and Sara obeyed immediately, scrambling up the steps like monkeys, bursting into loud, terrified wails as they gained the top. Anya could hear Betty Sue frantically shushing them, and then the sound of a door closing. She turned back to the dark man and the utter chill of his eyes. When he motioned her toward the living room, she went, forcing herself to keep her head up, her shaky legs steady. When he pointed at a chair, she sat down. He remained standing, the gun still part of his arm, staring at her.

"My name is Haman," he said abruptly. "I will tell you what to do. If you obey and we get what we want, no one will be hurt."

They all said that, and it meant nothing. She had read enough, seen enough on TV to know. It was part of the game. She lifted her chin. "I will bargain with you," she said. "Let the—the servant and the children go, and I will do what you ask."

This time Haman's smile held a tinge of amusement. "I do not ask. You will do as I say, whether we let them go or not. This is something you will learn. Now, where is the man Durant?"

Anya's heart jumped and began to pound. Was it Brady they were after? Was she the bait in a trap? "I don't know."

The black eyes narrowed. "I can make you tell the truth, Mrs. Meredith."

The sound of her name uttered in that odd cadence shocked her. He knew too much. "That is the truth," she said frozenly. "He—he travels."

A sound in the hall brought Anya's head around. Harry, and a blond woman in black jeans and fur-lined leather jacket. *Morgan.* A smiling Morgan, swinging toward her gaily. Morgan with Harry. Two members of The Game.

"Anya, darling! Brady's little revenge backfired, didn't it? He went too far . . ."

"Silence." Haman's calm voice chilled the silence he had asked for as he went on. "Why waste time? Now that we're all present, we can begin." He motioned for Anya to rise again. "I noted the telephone in the hall, Mrs. Meredith. You will use it to call Brady Durant, and I will tell you what to say."

"I can't." She got the words out of a paralyzed throat. "He has an unlisted number."

"I have it," Haman said. "Mrs. Whitcomb supplied it from her husband's files. Come. Shorten the time you must wait for freedom." Tension in his wiry frame belied his calm tone. He was impatient. Or uncertain?

Anya stole a glance at the clock. In forty-five minutes both Roger and Marilee would be driving up. There might be a chance then to get the children out. "It's no use," she said shakily. "Brady and I have—have parted. We quarreled. He will feel no obligation to me."

Morgan laughed. "That's an outright lie," she said contemptuously. "Brady is crazy about her, Haman. Like I said, this woman is your answer. She's the highest bid you can make."

Anya's head snapped around, her green eyes roving over Morgan's face incredulously. The highest bid! It was that damnable music box they wanted! And Morgan had set this up.

"*You*," she said softly. "After all Brady has done for you."

Morgan laughed again, the beautiful face bright with malice. "Only from guilt, darling. Mistaken guilt, I might add. Elisha was celebrating that night, not grieving. Anyway, Brady brought this on himself. Haman wants that stupid box, I don't. Harry and I are along for the fun."

"Enough." Haman moved rapidly between them. "Are you coming to the telephone, Mrs. Meredith, or shall I bring the children down and amuse myself with them while you make up your mind?"

Anya stared at him. He would do it. He would use those babies as a tool as casually as he would use his gun. It added fuel to her anger toward Morgan, a cold anger that temporarily erased her fear and sharpened her mind. She drew a deep breath and stood up. She had suddenly remembered that Brady had disconnected the telephone Saturday night and prayed that he hadn't reconnected it.

"You should have told me," she said, "that all you wanted was the music box. I would have cooperated immediately. Brady will part with it easily, for me. It's only a trinket." She smiled, hoping he would buy her new attitude as a real change of heart. But he was frowning, displeased.

"The Jacob Bruner masterpiece is not a trinket," he said frigidly. "It is—very valuable."

For once, there was emotion underlying his voice. The music box meant a great deal to him. Anya hid her surprise. "I know its value," she said stiffly. "It is not so valuable as a human life."

"It holds the value of many lives," Haman said roughly, and took her arm. "Mr. Durant will redeem them."

Anya shuddered inwardly from his touch as he led her to the hall. Taking the card he handed her, she tried to appear calm. Dialing, waiting for the first ring, she felt the phone lifted from her hand and looked up to see Haman holding it to his own ear. She could hear the trilling ring faintly, going on and on. Finally, Haman cradled the phone and frowned.

"We will try until he answers."

Anya nodded brightly. "I hope it's soon. I'd like to get this over with." Acting cooperative couldn't hurt. She glanced at the stairs, wishing she could tell Betty Sue to take any chance of getting the children out once Roger and Marilee appeared. But Haman took her arm again and led her back into the room with Harry and Morgan.

The Postons were close to a half hour late. They drove

up together, parking their cars in the yard, glanced curiously at the rusty white van, then linking arms, talking and laughing as they started up the walk.

"You know what to do," Harry said to Morgan. Morgan nodded, her face flaming with excitement, and ran out. Watching, standing well back from a window with Haman still clutching her arm, Anya saw Morgan rush toward Roger and Marilee and begin talking in an agitated manner, her small hands gesturing wildly, pushing back her hair, wiping her eyes.

Anya turned away with a small, broken sound. The dawning horror in Marilee's face and the frozen mask settling over Roger were harder to bear than her own deep fear. She pulled away from Haman's hand and went to sit in the chair he had chosen for her. His black eyes followed her, judging, impersonal. Then his eyes went to Harry with a hint of suspicion.

"Your partner is acting strangely," he said. "Why?"

Harry laughed uncomfortably. "Who knows? Morgan is a strange person."

Morgan's distraught mood was gone when she came back in. She strode in triumphantly. "They will stay in a car, where you can see them, Haman, and make no attempt to get help." She flung herself into a chair and beamed at Harry. "They bought our story, too. We are innocent hostages—caught here while visiting Anya." She chuckled. "They think I'm very brave to return to the house out of loyalty to you."

Haman swung toward her. "What story is this, Mrs. Whitcomb? You and Harry asked for the honor of assisting me!"

"We are assisting," Morgan said pertly. "Didn't you just see me doing my part? What difference does it make to you if they think us innocent? Be fair, Haman. We're with you all the way, but we aren't making a career of this. You said you would leave no incriminating witnesses, didn't you? When this is over, we intend to be solid citizens again."

"I see," Haman said, his dark face unreadable. "You wish to lead two lives. I should have brought Mahmoud, even at the risk of losing both of us." He glanced once more through the window, shrugged, and walked away. "Come," he said to Anya. "We will try the elusive Mr. Durant again." He went on toward the hall and then stopped, looking back at her unmoving figure. "Mrs. Meredith!"

Anya was very still, her eyes fixed in space, her thoughts fixed on one, incontrovertible fact. Haman meant to kill her once her usefulness was over. No incriminating witnesses. She was one, and so was Betty Sue. They might not even spare the children. *The children.* As Haman's patience wore thin, the danger to them increased. She stood up.

"I have a way to find Brady," Anya said stiffly. "It may take time, but he will call here. If you will allow the maid and the children to join the Postons in the car, I will do it."

"So, you've been holding out," Morgan said with relish. "I knew you'd break, Anya. Another half hour and you'll be begging to call Brady."

Anya hardly heard her. She was watching a killer's face darken with rage. "You will call now," Haman snarled, raising the gun. "I make no concessions."

Anya stared at the black mouth of the gun. "No, I won't," she said softly, and raised her eyes to his face. "What difference would a few hours make to me?"

The gun shifted, pointing at her breasts. "Do you know what this gun can do, Mrs. Meredith?"

She was past terror. She was in some bright, hollow world where words were more powerful than bullets. She smiled, feeling laughter rise in her throat.

"I know what it can't do," she said. "It can't call Brady Durant. It can't get your damnable music box for you. It can only kill, and I can only die once."

Across the room, Harry grunted with surprise and then laughed. "She's got you there, Haman. That's one gutsy woman."

Haman ignored him. His eyes, on Anya, were confused, uncertain. "It can kill children. The gun has no pity."

"Do you really think," Anya asked, "that if the gun killed children I would then call Mr. Durant?" Her smile was gone, her jaw set stubbornly. "You need me, Haman. You don't need the others."

The gun wavered. Then, slowly, Haman lowered it. His gaze left Anya and went to Morgan. "Mrs. Whitcomb, go upstairs and escort the maid and the children from the house. It is true that we need only this woman."

Morgan was on her feet, bristling. "That maid saw Harry, didn't she? What are you trying to do to us?"

"She saw only the gun," Haman said. "She was blind with terror. Now *go*." It was plain from his tone that he didn't care whether or not the maid could identify Harry.

"Not *me!*" Morgan's voice rose and cracked. "She never saw me! Send Harry."

Harry was looking hard at Haman, his heavy face full of suspicion. "She's right, you know," he said slowly. "That maid could cause us trouble. I don't like this. He got up, his heavy body suddenly menacing. "I don't like it at all."

Haman smiled. "Perhaps it is not necessary that you like it, Harry. You have become considerably less helpful since you decided to be a hostage." Somehow, Haman's gun now pointed at Harry's bulging waistline. Harry sat down abruptly.

"Well," he said, his red face losing color, "I'm not going up there, either. No use giving that maid another chance to look me over."

"Then I will do you a favor," Haman said smoothly. "I will make your new role more convincing." He walked over to Harry and held out his hand, the narrow palm up.

"Now, wait a minute," Harry blustered, "that's going too far..." Staring up at the dark face, he let his voice trail into silence. In a moment, he reached into a pocket and laid his gun in Haman's hand. "You're being a fool," he added weakly. "You may need me yet."

"I need no untrustworthy cowards," Haman said, pocketing the gun. "You and your playmate have achieved your goal. You are both hostages." His gaze swept over Morgan sardonically. "It would be wise to remember that you are no longer necessary in my plan. Don't antagonize me."

Anya had begun to breathe again, think again. She watched them all with growing amazement. Haman's slim, small figure emanated power, an inflexible will. Utter confidence. Both Harry and Morgan looked shocked, off-balance, like aging children caught in mischief. Now they were in as much danger as she was, and they knew it. Then Haman turned back to her and she stopped thinking of anyone else.

"It is regrettable that they haven't your courage," he said, "and even more regrettable that you do have it. However, I must make the best of it. You may bring down your hostages, Mrs. Meredith, and let them go."

She turned and ran, her long legs shaky. It was more than she had hoped for. She found them in a huddle in a back room, tear-streaked and miserable, with a clutter of pictures and scrawls of crayons.

"Your mommy and daddy are here," she said to the twins, "and they want you to come out to the car. Right now." She nodded at Betty Sue, agonized with fearful hope. "You are going, too. Bring the dogs." She watched the twins run out the door and turned back.

"Tell Mr. Poston that if Mr. Durant comes here, he must warn him. The man downstairs is a professional killer. Can you remember that?"

"Yes," Betty Sue whispered numbly. "It's—it's what I thought."

The twins were huddled halfway down the stairs, their heads down, waiting. They had seen Haman leaning against the open doorway, holding his gun. Anya urged them to their feet and down the rest of the steps. She could get none of them, even Betty Sue, to go any farther. She stepped away from them and stood in the doorway of the living room.

"Haman, if you will move over here with me—"

He looked at her incredulously, but he moved, quick and silent, watched as the children, dogs, and the young, pregnant woman fled through the door. Then he went to close and lock it.

"Why? There was space to spare."

Anya had followed him. She was watching through the pane of glass at the top of the door, seeing the car doors fly open, the twins rushing toward their parents. She saw Marilee drop to her knees, gathering her children in, saw Roger bending, stroking their bobbing heads, then standing to put a comforting arm around a sobbing Betty Sue. Anya shut her eyes for a moment. If she and Brady had had the chance, would they have had children? She sighed and turned back to Haman, answering his question.

"You have killed before."

"Many times," Haman said, not without pride. "But they do not know that."

"They smell it," Anya said gently. "So do I. Now, I suppose you will want to come with me upstairs. I have to find the number in one of my bags."

"I unpacked those bags," Haman said suspiciously. "There was nothing in them but clothes." He stared at her. "What does it smell like?"

"Death," Anya said. "Your own, perhaps. The number is in the clothes. In the pocket of some jeans."

"All women are confusing," Haman pronounced, following her up the stairs. "None more so than you Americans." His black eyes shone with a curious interest. "You were fearful at first, Mrs. Meredith. Now you are foolhardy enough to tell me I stink of death. That is an insult. Where did you find this courage?"

"I found it," Anya said, turning into her room, "when I realized you needed me." She looked at the open suitcases, the strewn clothes. "You didn't make this job any easier."

"I did not search well enough. I should have found the number." He sounded a bit disappointed. Watching her kneel and begin sorting, he went on. "When I no longer need you, will you be so brave?"

"No, I will not." Rummaging in pockets, Anya thought with distant humor that she was beginning to talk like Haman. "I have never been brave. I'm afraid of everything. That gun you have—it makes my blood freeze."

Haman laughed and patted the boxlike side. "A fine gun, Mrs. Meredith. An Uzi. It can cut a car in two—very fast, very efficiently."

"Here it is," Anya said, bringing out a piece of paper. "Crumpled, but I can read it. Cutting a car in two doesn't sound very useful. How often do you find someone who wants a car cut in two?" All right, she *was* losing her mind. It seemed forgivable, right now. She watched, frozen with doubt, as Haman snatched the piece of paper from her fingers. Was she only bringing Brady to his death, too? Why did she think he could save them all? Because she did, for a moment there, she really did think he could. Brady was a better man than this one. But that gun . . .

"A toll number," Haman said, studying the paper. "Very strange. You are sure of this number?"

"Toll free," Anya corrected automatically. "Yes, I am sure. It's a sort of central exchange—they find him and he calls back. Or so he said. I'll try it." She pushed herself up from her knees, the effort reminding her of how little sleep she had had and how tired she was. She headed for the stairs and the telephone down the hall.

"The point in cutting a car in two," Haman said behind her, "is to kill your enemies who are riding inside. It is often done in the Middle East."

Chapter 15

WHILE ANYA DIALED, Haman brought the phone to her ear, holding it loosely, placing his head against hers so that they could both hear. His breath stirred her hair and Anya steeled herself against the stomach-wrenching revulsion that came close to choking her. The woman answering on the other end of the line was cool and efficient.

"Name, please."

"Anya Meredith."

"Contact?"

"Brady Durant."

"Number?"

"Number?" Anya was confused. Did Brady have a number? Was this some kind of a test?

"The number," the woman said patronizingly, "that you want him to call."

"Oh." Looking down, Anya read the number from the Poston phone and then listened as the woman repeated it. "That's it," she said, relieved, and heard the other phone click down. She drew away as Haman replaced the one they had been using.

"You did well," he said. "You said nothing to cause suspicion. However, the clerk gave no indication of when the call would be made."

"Perhaps she doesn't know. After all, they have to find him . . ." She jumped, startled, as the telephone rang.

Haman's hand shot past her and picked up the phone. "Yes, she is here." He was very careful to sound as American as possible, but the same subtle cadence was

169

there. "Who is calling, please? Mr. Durant? I will find her." He had trouble with the name, always. It came out "Dahrawn." But from the look in his glittering, excited eyes, he was satisfied with himself. He put his palm over the mouthpiece and gave instructions.

"You will say where you are. You will say it is necessary that he bring the music box here. You will also say that if he comes alone there will be no trouble, but if he brings the police many will die." The black eyes fixed on hers. "All will die. In spite of your efforts, the car will be no protection for the others."

Anya heard every word, but she was conscious of two other things. Brady was on the end of this line, and, after she had completed what she had to say, she might have only minutes to live. It might be the last chance to tell him anything.

"I will say what you told me to say, and I will tell him I trust him to do it. And should I mention the Poston family? Brady is fond of them and he wouldn't want them harmed."

Haman smiled. "An excellent thought. Mention the children. Americans are very soft in regard to children. But nothing more, Mrs. Meredith."

She nodded and took the phone, swallowing. "Brady?"

The tense "yes" in his deep voice rocked her heart, brought tears to her eyes. One of the last words she would ever hear him say? She swallowed again, looking up at Haman.

"I am at the Poston home. You must bring the music box here. If you come alone there will be no trouble, but if you bring police many will die. The Postons are outside with the twins. They are in a car—which is no protection. I trust you." Then, because it was the last chance and because she loved him, she went on without hesitation. "One man with an Uzi."

Haman slapped her, hard, across the mouth, knocking the telephone from her hand, sending her and the light chair toppling over backward. He grabbed the telephone and spoke into it harshly. "She will be the first to die if you don't obey." He slammed the phone down and jerked Anya to her feet.

"I should kill you now! You could have done nothing worse than to give away my lack of strength!" He slapped her again, a sharp blow across her cheek that would have knocked her sprawling if he hadn't been holding her. Then he pushed her in front of him into the living room and threw her into a chair. Harry and Morgan stared at her numbly as she straightened and leaned back, her face clearly marked by a red image of Haman's hand.

Harry cleared his throat and looked at Haman. "What did she do?"

"She warned him," Haman said bitterly, stalking toward a window. "She told him there was only one armed man."

"You can fix that," Harry said eagerly. "Give me back my pistol."

Haman turned, sneering. "And have you shoot me in the back to prove yourself a hero?" He stood glaring at the two of them, at Harry's purpling face, at Morgan huddled, frightened, in her chair. *"Leave,"* he said, suddenly vicious. "Leave while I'm fool enough to let you live. Take the plumber's truck. It is of no use to me."

They were on their feet, moving rapidly toward the door, Morgan keeping Harry's bulk between her and the gun. "We won't say anything to anyone," Harry was saying earnestly. "We'll wait at the camp with the others. This is all a mistake, Haman."

"Yes," Haman said, following them. "Mine. I mistook you for a man."

Anya could see them from her chair as they hastily unlocked the door and hurried out while Haman stood watching in the open doorway. She would now be alone in the house with Haman, but it seemed no more dangerous, nor less. As Haman came back into the room, she looked at him curiously.

"They may inform the police."

"They won't dare," Haman said contemptuously. "You are still alive to testify against them." He stood looking down at her, nervously fingering the trigger of the gun. "When will this man Durant arrive?"

"I don't know." She saw the quick anger, and added, "I don't know where he was. A toll-free number tells me nothing. He could be here in an hour or a day." She leaned back again, closing her eyes against the sight of the dark face. "I can only tell you he will be here as quickly as he can." She heard Haman move away, a whisper of air in the silence, receding toward the window.

It was, according to the living room clock, a little less than two hours. They both heard the noise of an approaching vehicle and both were on their feet, standing back but looking through a window as a Jeep drove up the incline. A dull green Jeep like a million others, enclosed with curtains against the cold wind. It slowed, circled, and came to a stop pointing downhill toward the highway. The door opened, and Brady got out, his tall figure erect, moving easily across the space to the Postons' car.

Anya could hear her own labored breathing. A wave of love and fear swept over her at sight of him, making her eyes blur, her body tremble. She watched him leaning on the Postons' car, talking and listening. Then he straightened and began walking toward the house. All at once, she bitterly regretted calling him, bringing him here. She wanted to scream to him to go back, get in the Jeep and leave. She lunged toward the window and Haman's hand snaked out and caught her.

"Let him come. He wishes to speak." The black eyes were glittering again, excited.

Brady stopped midway of the walk, his eyes scanning the windows. "I want to see Anya Meredith," he called, *"now."*

Haman swept aside the sheer curtains, grabbed Anya, and thrust her against the glass, putting his gun in plain view beside her.

"She is still alive, Durant. She will stay alive if you have followed my instructions."

Brady's rock-hard face wore a look of agony as he stared at Anya, and then tightened again. Slowly, he removed his jacket and tossed it on the grass. He raised his arms, showing as the shirt stretched across his powerful torso that he was hiding no weapon. Then, turning around, he pulled out all his pockets and left them dangling, spreading his empty hands.

"He is very efficient," Haman said approvingly. "Very careful." He raised his voice. "Where is the Bruner box?"

Brady moved closer. "In the Jeep. The Jeep is full of gas and running. Leave the woman there and come out. No one will interfere. No one is waiting."

Haman laughed. "Do you take me for a fool? Get the box out, open it! Stand there, ready to hand it to me. I will bring the woman to you."

And past you, Anya thought dully. Into the Jeep. And, somewhere along the way back into the forest, when Haman was sure no cordon of police waited, that would be the end of it. Brady had moved even closer to the window, and she searched his face hungrily, wishing she could see his eyes clearly. Wishing she could tell him once more that she loved him. Tell him to be careful. Then he was nodding, turning back to the Jeep.

"He's going to do it," Haman muttered, excited again. "What else can he do? A sensible man." He laughed again, a high, almost hysterical sound. "Not fortunate, in this case, but sensible." He dragged Anya from the window and let the curtain fall. "Come," he said, "we are going out. A man as sensible as he is would not lie about the Irade."

The Irade? The music box. For a brief second Anya felt hysteria rising in her own throat. That damned, unmusical music box had brought them all to the brink of death. *Why?*

When the door was unlocked and they stepped outside, Brady was standing beside the walk with the music box glittering in his hand, open to show the red velvet interior. She could see his hair blowing in the breeze; she could see with a trembling satisfaction that the Postons' car was empty, the doors on the far side open. Brady had known what she meant, and he had warned them. They would have slipped out and over the slope of the ravine. She could only hope that Haman would keep his eyes on Brady. She could hear Haman's fast breathing, feel it in the pressure of the gun barrel on her back.

"Walk slowly," Haman whispered. "Move only when the gun pushes you. Otherwise, I may think you are trying to escape."

Anya nodded, her tangled hair falling around her cheeks, her huge eyes fastened on Brady, memorizing, loving. There would be nothing he could do while Haman held her like this. One move, and the gun would blast them both. Brady would know about the gun. He would be—sensible.

Closer, now. And she could see his eyes at last. Those blue, blue eyes, so ridiculously beautiful in his rugged face. She drew in her breath sharply, wobbling, catching her balance. *Brady meant to try! It was impossible, but he meant to try!* She could see it in his eyes. Blue steel. Rigid with fear, she stared at him, hoping he would understand that they would both be dead in seconds. But the steel determination stayed as she watched. She could almost feel the taut muscles of the body she knew so well, feel the readiness, the poised sword of his anger.

"It's beautiful, a fitting receptacle." Haman's voice, strangely soft, breathing appreciation. His hand reached out and touched her shoulder, bringing her to a stop as they came abreast of Brady. The barrel of the Uzi dug into her back, a merciless reminder as he spoke again.

"I wish to hear it, Mr. Durant. I must be sure it isn't a clever copy."

Brady raised his left hand and turned the carved rose, dropping the hand again and extending his right arm, holding the box closer to Haman so he could hear the tinny tinkle.

Facing forward, Anya could now see nothing of Brady but his left side, the strong, muscled leg, the dangling hand. Which was moving. Moving very slowly, imperceptibly aiming at a point between Haman and her, a point where a gun barrel pressed against her back. She wanted to scream. She wanted to reach out, push the hand down, hold it there. Then, suddenly, she knew Brady could do it. With luck. With a tiny bit of luck . . .

"Ah, yes," Haman said softly behind her, "you have not tried to fool me. It is the Irade, at last. The Irade itself." He sounded almost reverent. Anya felt the pressure of the gun ease slightly as Haman reached for the box, saw Brady's slow moving hand blur into speed, and she flung herself forward on the brick walk, hearing the ear-splitting, stuttering roar as the Uzi exploded into action, spitting its sure death harmlessly into an open sky. She rolled, scrambling away from the struggling men, seeing Brady's powerful arm high in the air, his big hand wrapped around the thin dark fingers and stuttering gun, his strength lifting Haman clear of the ground. The slim, wiry body twisted and kicked viciously; a stream of curses poured from Haman's contorted mouth. Then Brady's fist smashed into the dark face and Haman dropped, going to his knees, scrabbling frantically in the grass beside the walk. Anya gasped as she saw him grab the fallen silver box and, crouching, run for the Jeep. Jumping in, he roared away down the incline.

Numbly, Anya sat up, raising her eyes to the tall man towering over her. He was still holding the gun, looking down at her bruised face with his heart in his blue eyes. He hefted the gun, tossed it aside, and sat down on the walk with her, gathering her into his arms.

"I've been criminally stupid," he said bitterly. "Can you ever forgive me?"

"That should be easy," Anya quavered. "You just saved my life." Then she burst into tears, into gulping sobs she couldn't stop. Burrowing into his warmth, feeling his arms tight around her, she knew she was alive, loved, saved. But the sobs kept coming, in spite of what seemed an enormous crowd of people coming up, circling, making comforting sounds.

"Let her cry," Brady said. "She's been through hell." He picked her up and carried her into the house and up the stairs, finding her room easily since it was the one with clothes strewn all over it. Marilee followed, pale and shaken.

"I'll stay with her," she said. "There's a man downstairs who says he's a friend of yours and wants to talk to you. He—he came running out of the woods with a rifle."

"Tell him to wait," Brady said. "I'm staying with Anya."

An hour later, he brought her downstairs, pale but with a luminous smile. They stepped through a clutter of children on the hall floor and went into the living room. Anya winced when she saw the tall, expressionless man waiting with Roger and Marilee. She never wanted to think of the Bruner box again.

"I feel fine," she said in answer to Marilee's murmured question, "except I'm starving."

"That can wait," Marilee said heartlessly, "until I find out what's been going on. That—that terrorist got away scot-free, and no one has even called the police."

Brady looked at the poker-faced stranger. "Either you tell them or I will. They won't talk, and they deserve to know." He sat down on the couch, pulling Anya with him. "This is Tom Galway, of the CIA. He's had the box ever since I took it away from Morgan."

In the shocked silence, Marilee spoke indignantly. "Well, he doesn't have it now. That crook has it. It ought to be reported—"

"We want him to have it," Galway said. "Let me give it to you fast. A month from now, Haman and Mahmoud will lead a group of renegade survivalists in an attack on a main transportation center in the United States. We know the place, we know the hour, and we will be waiting. It's our chance to capture and convict them all." He paused, enjoying the shocked attention. "They will be following instructions contained in the music box."

"But there was nothing in the box," Anya said wonderingly. "It had a secret compartment, but it was empty."

Galway flushed. "It was hard to find. When Durant brought the box to us, intending to sell it, we asked him to help. He agreed to wait a few days while we found the message and decoded it, then sell it to Mrs. Whitcomb. We knew she'd give it to Haman and we could sit back and wait for the right day. Believe me, we took that box apart—looking for microfilm, microdots, anything. We found nothing. Yet we had good information; we knew it was there, so we kept looking. Durant was forced into the position of withholding the box when Whitcomb told the outlaws he had it, and that brought on this trouble today. Thank God, we found and decoded the message Saturday, so it all worked out. But—well, it could have been tragic except for Durant. I'm extremely sorry, Mrs. Meredith."

"Well," Marilee demanded, "where *was* the message? In the mechanism? That was the only hidden spot."

Galway shook his head. "In the music. One of our men finally decided it was too bad to be real and tested it. Recorded and slowed down, it's a long and detailed plan. Chanted, by the way, in a Muslim language. They call it an Irade, an order that must be obeyed. The followers hold it sacred. Some ancient superstition the top terrorists have turned to their own purposes."

"Chopin would have hated it," Anya said. "It was awful."

"But useful," Galway answered, "as you'll see next month in the national news." He stood up and reached for his long coat. "I don't need to tell you, of course . . ."

"You certainly don't," Marilee said firmly. "Even I can keep my mouth shut when there's a good reason."

"We're leaving, too," Brady said, and stood, bringing Anya up with him. "Any more talk can wait. Anya's exhausted."

"And hungry," Marilee said quickly. "Stay for dinner."

"We'll have dinner in Dahlonega," Brady answered, and headed for the hall. "I'll bring down your bags, love."

Anya smiled at Marilee and shrugged. "He stuck me in the shower, and when I came out my bags were all packed. I guess I'm moving, after all."

"I'm a painter again," Brady said, driving through the long lane that led to his house. "Not an amateur secret agent." He reached out, enveloping Anya's hand in his, caressing her wrist with his thumb. "No more meetings with the CIA, no more trying to hide my woman so she won't get kidnaped. Thank God, it's finally over."

Anya glanced at him. He looked ridiculously large in her little car, but she didn't mind that. She was thankful for his size and strength. And the quickness of his hands. "Was that what you were doing? Hiding me?"

"Trying to. But I should have known Morgan would eventually lead those rats to you. For revenge, if nothing else."

Anya sighed. She had told him most of what had happened while they drove to Dahlonega and had dinner, and now she didn't want to think about it. The criminals had what they wanted, and maybe she had what she wanted, too. She looked up as the car swung through the maple grove and came to a stop. She stepped out, raising her face to the night sky, looking at the stars and breathing in the scent of pines. The broad lines of the house were like welcoming arms, stretching to fold her in.

"Hide me here," she said softly, "where no one can find me." She looked at him and laughed. "Except the CIA, of course. No wonder the state police were so cooperative with Galway."

"Galway won't be looking for us," Brady said, gathering up her bags. "He's somewhat embarrassed about the danger he put you in." He grinned suddenly. "Himself, too. He was hiding in a tree near the house with that rifle when the Uzi went off. It clipped away a branch right over his head. He took it home with him."

"The branch?"

Brady chuckled. "The Uzi. You are tired, love. Come on, I'll put you to bed."

A single low light burned in the bedroom upstairs, illuminating the nearest two of the paintings that lined the walls, casting a golden light on the dove-gray walls. Anya could see only part of the glow; the rest was obliterated by the arch of Brady's chest, rising and falling in deep, even breathing beside her. The glow seemed very like the feeling she had inside, a warm, golden feeling of solid happiness.

"Brady?"

His arm tightened around her. "Hmm?"

"I'm not a coward."

He turned toward her, his grin a flash in the dim light. "I never thought you were."

"I did." She stretched luxuriously against his warm side, running a slender foot along his hairy leg in sensual enjoyment. "But I'm not."

He turned farther, putting his other arm around her, holding her close. "You saw the face of the enemy, love."

She lay very still, remembering. "Yes. That was it. I had to be brave. And," she added, shyly proud, "I was. I feel better about myself, knowing I can be brave when it's necessary."

He kissed her smooth forehead, her cheek, his mouth moving slowly along the delicate line of her jaw. "If I start feeling better about you," he murmured, "you won't get any sleep." They had made love, gentle, tender love, when they had first gotten into bed, but she wasn't surprised by his quickening body. She moved close, trailing a hand along his muscular side.

"I can sleep tomorrow."

"Ah, darling..." He pressed against her, his hand

running over her slender body, shaping it, memorizing the curves. "How I do love you. Are you going to marry me, Annie Anya?"

"Of course," she said, raising her arms, circling his neck. "Haven't I told you I'm a very brave woman?"

Second Chance at Love ®

___ 0-425-08151-6	GENTLEMAN AT HEART #263 Elissa Curry	$2.25
___ 0-425-08152-4	BY LOVE POSSESSED #264 Linda Barlow	$2.25
___ 0-425-08153-2	WILDFIRE #265 Kelly Adams	$2.25
___ 0-425-08154-0	PASSION'S DANCE #266 Lauren Fox	$2.25
___ 0-425-08155-9	VENETIAN SUNRISE #267 Kate Nevins	$2.25
___ 0-425-08199-0	THE STEELE TRAP #268 Betsy Osborne	$2.25
___ 0-425-08200-8	LOVE PLAY #269 Carole Buck	$2.25
___ 0-425-08201-6	CAN'T SAY NO #270 Jeanne Grant	$2.25
___ 0-425-08202-4	A LITTLE NIGHT MUSIC #271 Lee Williams	$2.25
___ 0-425-08203-2	A BIT OF DARING #272 Mary Haskell	$2.25
___ 0-425-08204-0	THIEF OF HEARTS #273 Jan Mathews	$2.25
___ 0-425-08284-9	MASTER TOUCH #274 Jasmine Craig	$2.25
___ 0-425-08285-7	NIGHT OF A THOUSAND STARS #275 Petra Diamond	$2.25
___ 0-425-08286-5	UNDERCOVER KISSES #276 Laine Allen	$2.25
___ 0-425-08287-3	MAN TROUBLE #277 Elizabeth Henry	$2.25
___ 0-425-08288-1	SUDDENLY THAT SUMMER #278 Jennifer Rose	$2.25
___ 0-425-08289-X	SWEET ENCHANTMENT #279 Diana Mars	$2.25
___ 0-425-08461-2	SUCH ROUGH SPLENDOR #280 Cinda Richards	$2.25
___ 0-425-08462-0	WINDFLAME #281 Sarah Crewe	$2.25
___ 0-425-08463-9	STORM AND STARLIGHT #282 Lauren Fox	$2.25
___ 0-425-08464-7	HEART OF THE HUNTER #283 Liz Grady	$2.25
___ 0-425-08465-5	LUCKY'S WOMAN #284 Delaney Devers	$2.25
___ 0-425-08466-3	PORTRAIT OF A LADY #285 Elizabeth N. Kary	$2.25
___ 0-425-08508-2	ANYTHING GOES #286 Diana Morgan	$2.25
___ 0-425-08509-0	SOPHISTICATED LADY #287 Elissa Curry	$2.25
___ 0-425-08510-4	THE PHOENIX HEART #288 Betsy Osborne	$2.25
___ 0-425-08511-2	FALLEN ANGEL #289 Carole Buck	$2.25
___ 0-425-08512-0	THE SWEETHEART TRUST #290 Hilary Cole	$2.25
___ 0-425-08513-9	DEAR HEART #291 Lee Williams	$2.25
___ 0-425-08514-7	SUNLIGHT AND SILVER #292 Kelly Adams	$2.25
___ 0-425-08515-5	PINK SATIN #293 Jeanne Grant	$2.25
___ 0-425-08516-3	FORBIDDEN DREAM #294 Karen Keast	$2.25
___ 0-425-08517-1	LOVE WITH A PROPER STRANGER #295 Christa Merlin	$2.25
___ 0-425-08518-X	FORTUNE'S DARLING #296 Frances Davies	$2.25
___ 0-425-08519-8	LUCKY IN LOVE #297 Jacqueline Topaz	$2.25

Prices may be slightly higher in Canada.

COMING NEXT MONTH
IN THE
SECOND CHANCE AT LOVE SERIES

QUESTIONNAIRE

1. How do you rate _____
                          (please print TITLE)
   - ☐ excellent   ☐ good
   - ☐ very good   ☐ fair   ☐ poor

2. How likely are you to purchase another book in this series?
   - ☐ definitely would purchase
   - ☐ probably would purchase
   - ☐ probably would not purchase
   - ☐ definitely would not purchase

3. How likely are you to purchase another book by this author?
   - ☐ definitely would purchase
   - ☐ probably would purchase
   - ☐ probably would not purchase
   - ☐ definitely would not purchase

4. How does this book compare to books in other contemporary romance lines?
   - ☐ much better
   - ☐ better
   - ☐ about the same
   - ☐ not as good
   - ☐ definitely not as good

5. Why did you buy this book? (Check as many as apply)
   - ☐ I have read other SECOND CHANCE AT LOVE romances
   - ☐ friend's recommendation
   - ☐ bookseller's recommendation
   - ☐ art on the front cover
   - ☐ description of the plot on the back cover
   - ☐ book review I read
   - ☐ other _____
     _____
     _____

(Continued...)

6. Please list your three favorite contemporary romance lines.

_____
_____

7. Please list your favorite authors of contemporary romance lines.

_____
_____
_____
_____
_____
_____

8. How many SECOND CHANCE AT LOVE romances have you read? _____

9. How many series romances like SECOND CHANCE AT LOVE do you <u>read</u> each month? _____

10. How many series romances like SECOND CHANCE AT LOVE do you <u>buy</u> each month? _____

11. Mind telling your age?
    ☐ under 18
    ☐ 18 to 30
    ☐ 31 to 45
    ☐ over 45

☐ Please check if you'd like to receive our <u>free</u> SECOND CHANCE AT LOVE Newsletter.

We hope you'll share your other ideas about romances with us on an additional sheet and attach it securely to this questionnaire.

• •

Fill in your name and address below:
Name _____
Street Address _____
City _____ State _____ Zip _____

Please return this questionnaire to:
   SECOND CHANCE AT LOVE
   The Berkley Publishing Group
   200 Madison Avenue, New York, New York 10016